FLight 171

FLIGHT 171

AMY CHRISTINE PARKER

Underlined

Text copyright © 2022 by Amy Christine Parker
Cover photo © 2022 by zheng long/Stocksy

Underlined is a registered trademark and the colophon is a trademark of Penguin Random House LLC.

Visit us on the Web! GetUnderlined.com

Educators and librarians, for a variety of teaching tools, visit us at RHTeachersLibrarians.com

Library of Congress Cataloging-in-Publication Data is available upon request.
ISBN 978-0-593-56303-8 (trade pbk.) — ISBN 978-0-593-56304-5 (ebook)

The text of this book is set in 11.3-point Adobe Garamond.
Interior design by Cathy Bobak

Printed in the United States of America
10 9 8 7 6 5 4 3 2 1
First Edition

To Jay, Sammi, and Riley for never losing faith,
even when I did

HOUR ONE

CHAPTER 1

"SO, CLASS TRIP POLL: IF YOU HAD TO CHOOSE BETWEEN DYING in a plane crash or a car accident, which would you pick?" Spencer nudges my back with his elbow as we make our way down the Jetway toward our plane. He has a Twizzler hanging out of his mouth and a wiseass grin on his beefy face.

Resist the urge to turn around and kick him in the shin, I silently tell myself. Sometimes he can be so totally clueless.

Outside the tiny Jetway window is the nose of the Sky Royal airplane we're about to board. Rain runs in rivulets down the glass, making the plane look like it's submerged in water. I can barely make out the blurry outlines of the pilots inside the cockpit. The night is dark and full of gathering storm clouds. No lightning yet, but the sky is ominous enough that I can't help wondering if our takeoff will be delayed. Part of me hopes it is. I'm still not sure if it's a good idea for me to go on this trip.

"Yeah, Devon, which would you choose? Plane or car?"

I look past Spencer to Billy, his partner in crime and fellow wrestler on the Greendale team. He reaches up to touch the ceiling of the Jetway with both hands, making sure to flex his biceps as he does. Glancing down at his midsection, he adjusts slightly so his six-pack is clearly visible through his T-shirt. Then he looks up at me, one eyebrow raised like he's expecting me to react more to his body than to the question. "Inquiring minds want to know."

"Don't be such utter tools, you two." My friend Kiara rolls her eyes and reaches around me to punch both boys' biceps hard, first Spencer's, then Billy's.

"Ow!" Spencer rubs his arm.

Kiara points a finger at him. "What kind of question is that? *After Emily—the hit-and-run.*" Her voice drops to a whisper when she says my dead twin's name, then goes back up to full volume. "And, considering we're all about to board a plane, it's bad luck to talk about crashing."

Spencer's smile falters. He darts a look at me, then chews on his Twizzler more vigorously until half of it disappears into his mouth.

I drop to one knee and start to pretend-tie my shoe. I let my hair form a curtain over my face so I don't have to see Kiara and the boys give me anxious looks. I'm not gonna lose it over one stupid comment. Still, Emily's face floats unbidden through my mind, the way she looked at me that last time, just before her accident. I didn't know it would be the last time. If I had, I wouldn't have done or said what I did.

My throat gets tight. It's hard to swallow around the lump

lodged there. I need my drumsticks. Badly. The old me kept them handy for moments like this, when life was weird or awkward or just plain unbearable. I'd bang out a rhythm on the nearest hard surface until whatever anxiety I was feeling left my body by way of my hands and the beat. But that was before last October. Halloween night.

I don't play the drums anymore.

I tuck my hands inside my pockets to remind my body of this. Still, there's the echo of a series of rhythms rolling through my head like an itch in a phantom limb.

To my right, the door to the Jetway slams open. A baggage handler wearing a safety vest slips inside, letting a blast of cool March air rush toward us. He shakes the raindrops from his hair, then grabs a pair of strollers from beside the door and ducks back outside. The sudden drop in temperature makes me shiver violently, but it's good, bracing enough to make the tears building in my eyes dry up.

When I stand, Spencer's eyes lock on mine and he winces. "Devon. I'm sorry. I forgot about . . . God, I guess I wasn't thinking."

Of course he wasn't. Thinking isn't one of Spencer's strong suits. He's the guy who fits the dumb-jock cliché perfectly—or at least he willingly feeds into it.

"Yeah, me too," Billy says softly. He lets his arms drop and stuffs his hands into his pockets.

Kiara glares at them one last time before stepping back into line in front of me.

"Devon, seriously." Spencer touches my hand tentatively. "I really am sorry. Hey, want a Twizzler?" He shakes the oversized candy bag at me.

"Thanks." I take one piece so he'll leave me alone, and nibble on the end. The flight must be crowded, because we're moving down the Jetway at a snail's pace.

I'm not okay, not really. I'm tired of everyone treading so lightly around me ever since Emily was hit by a car and died. Nearly five months have gone by, and people still look at me with sad eyes, watching me like I'm a land mine set to either explode or break down. It makes working through things harder. All the constant sympathetic comments are like fingernails picking at a freshly formed scab, making the wound raw all over again. It doesn't help that the person who hit my sister hasn't been caught—that no matter how hard I try to find them, I keep hitting dead ends.

I glance at my watch. It's nearly midnight. Soon we'll be airborne. I get a squirmy, uncomfortable feeling in the pit of my stomach.

Am I really going on the senior class ski trip without my sister?

When Mr. Lewton announced it earlier this school year, Emily and I attended the planning meeting together. Now she's gone. And I'm going alone.

I take a deep breath and hike my backpack higher on my shoulder. Time to think about something else, anything else. I glance at the back of the line.

Jack is there.

Oh, God.

All at once my stomach is a roller coaster rocketing through a loop-de-loop.

He wasn't supposed to come. He hasn't been to any of the trip planning meetings. He's been homeschooling since the end of last year—since Halloween. I haven't even seen him around town— not since I accused him of killing my sister.

I still think he did it. I just can't figure out how to prove it.

Kiara tugs at my arm.

"Don't. Ignore him." It's part plea, part command.

Jack has his earbuds in and is tapping his phone screen. His hair—the exact shade of chestnuts—flops over his face, obscuring his eyes. He hasn't noticed me noticing him yet. My brain automatically fills in the details of his face. Deep brown eyes with little yellow flecks, framed by thick eyebrows that curve upward when he's curious about something or someone. The barely-there constellation of freckles that border his jawline and forehead. I spent so much of last summer and fall memorizing the angles and planes of his face, the way they set my heart beating in an entirely new rhythm—one that was all stuttering staccato beats. Until Halloween. Until Emily, when the beats changed. Got harder, vengeful. Full of anger.

I sort of want him to look up. To notice me standing here watching him. Just because the police ruled him out as a suspect doesn't mean I've given up. I won't let it go, not until I am one hundred percent certain he wasn't driving the car that hit Emily. I hang on to the flame of anger seeing him ignites in me . . . because there is a traitor part of me, one I can't seem to squash no matter how hard I try, who still looks at him with longing. And I hate myself for it.

"God, I wish they'd hurry up already. What is taking so long?" Kiara heaves a sigh and picks a piece of lint off her wool coat before she side-eyes me. "You all right?"

"Yep," I lie.

She tucks her long black hair behind her ears and narrows her eyes. "You sure? 'Cause if you're not, it's okay to back out of this trip. I mean, we aren't on the plane just yet."

Now that I've seen Jack, part of me *does* want to back out. I'm only on this trip because my parents want me to focus on something fun, something normal for a change—anything other than the person who killed my twin. How am I supposed to do that with him around?

"Well?" Kiara asks.

I take one last look at the little patch of airport I can make out at the other end of the Jetway. I could just leave my place in line, call Dad, and ask him to pick me up . . . but my mom is already on the plane with the rest of the flight crew. She rearranged her whole schedule to be here. She'll be disappointed if I don't go through with this trip. And I made a promise to myself after Emily, after what I did Halloween night, that I wouldn't disappoint either of my parents again. They've been through too much to have to endure anything else.

"No way I'm missing this," I say, making my voice as Emily-esque as I can manage, all buoyant cheer. I've gotten pretty good at sounding and looking like her these days, of banishing what's left of the old me. If either of us had to die, it should've been me, not her. Since that didn't happen, I figure the second-best thing is for me to become more like her and be less like myself, give my parents back some version of the better daughter.

Kiara pats my back gently, then straightens the scarf around her neck until it's perfectly draped. She hates when anything is out of place.

"Colorado, here we come," she squeals.

I take a deep breath and step off the Jetway and onto the plane.

CHAPTER 2

MOM IS IN THE BUSINESS CLASS GALLEY WITH THE FLIGHT CREW. Her eyes light up when she sees me.

"There you are. I was beginning to wonder if you'd changed your mind." Her smile slips just a little.

I get it. I haven't always been good at keeping promises . . . or doing what my parents ask me to.

"We had to make one last bathroom run, Mrs. Marsh." Kiara leans in to hug my mother. "Thank you for helping us get such a great deal on this flight."

"Well, given it's a red-eye, it wasn't all that hard," Mom says, beaming. "And I might have the inside scoop on all the best deals."

"*And* it's the first flight on Friday the thirteenth, so of course it was a good deal," Billy says, crowding onto the plane. "Not exactly the luckiest day to fly, is it?"

"Technically, it's still the twelfth," Kiara argues.

Billy glances at his phone. "Yeah, for about ten more minutes."

"Hey, aren't you supposed to be in the cockpit, Mrs. Marsh?" Spencer asks. "I mean, you're the pilot, right?"

"Not for this flight," I say. "She's deadheading from Denver to Los Angeles."

Spencer looks confused. "Deadheading?"

"Traveling to my next assignment," Mom says.

"But why not fly this one, too?" Billy asks.

"It's safety protocol. All pilots have restrictions on how many hours they can fly. We can't afford to be tired in there," Mom explains patiently as she gestures to the cockpit. "So I'll be napping through this flight to make sure I'm fresh for tomorrow." She locks eyes with me and winks. "I'm mainly here for moral support."

Translation: she wanted to make sure I got on the plane. Or maybe she knew that Jack was going on the trip and wanted to make sure I didn't confront him about Emily again. But it's been more than three months since that happened. I'm calmer now. I've changed. I'm more like my twin. I won't confront Jack again until I have incontrovertible proof.

Obviously my mom still doesn't believe that the changes I've made will stick.

"Devon, you remember Shazia, right?" Mom gestures to the flight attendant standing next to her wearing a hijab the same shade of red as her uniform blouse. "From the Sky Royal launch event?"

"Of course," I lie. The launch event happened a month after Emily died. I barely remembered how to breathe back then.

"Good to see you again, Devon." Shazia turns toward the man in front of Kiara and me. He's holding a very squirmy, very cute little boy with a mop of curly hair who is noisily sucking his thumb.

"Aren't you the cutest?" Shazia plays peekaboo with him, and he smiles shyly around his thumb.

"He just turned three last week," his father says, more than a hint of pride in his voice.

"Well, happy birthday." Shazia holds up a miniature airplane and the boy takes it. "That's my last one, so hold it tight."

"What do you say, Kamal?" his father prompts.

"Thank you," Kamal whispers. He begins moving the plane in the air and making whooshing noises.

Without a word, Kiara moves deftly around the boy and his dad into business class. She's not one for standing still any longer than necessary.

Before I can follow, Mom eyes my clothes: Emily's cornflower-blue sweater with one of her white long-sleeved tees underneath and a pair of jeans. I even straightened the waves out of my hair, just like Emily used to.

Mom's eyes get shiny. She gives me a quick, intense hug. "Try to have fun this week, okay? Let go a little." Her fingers press against my shoulder blades and then release. What she doesn't say but I'm certain is implied is: *leave Jack alone.* Except I'm already turning and seeking him out. I can't seem to stop myself.

"I'll be in the crew bunk room if you need me. Shazia can let you in with her ID card," Mom says.

But I'm still too busy looking for Jack to listen closely to what she's saying. I can't see him anymore; people are crowded too tightly around the door.

Wait.

There he is, attempting to hide behind a middle-aged guy, furtively watching me.

I whirl around fast, too fast. I must pick my foot up weird, because the heel of my boot catches on some uneven bit of the galley floor. I lose my balance and accidentally crash into Kamal and his dad.

"Oh!" Kamal's dad stumbles into the wall. The toy airplane flies out of Kamal's hands and clatters to the floor.

"No! It crashed!" Kamal hollers.

"I'm so sorry," I blurt, feeling my face heat up. "I tripped."

Kamal starts to cry. He leans over to reach for the plane.

I hurry past, still muttering sorrys, my hands fisted tightly around my backpack straps. I can feel Mom watching me, the heaviness of her constant concern weighing me down. Every move I make—accidental or otherwise—is worthy of dissection. She lost one daughter and now she'll be hell-bound before she loses the other. I actually heard her say these words to my dad a few weeks ago. I'm not sure what she thinks I'm at risk of—letting my guilt get the best of me? Doing something dangerous because of it? Well, I won't. That's why I'm trying to be more like Emily. I hate that they think I'd be that rash.

"That could've gone smoother," Kiara says when I catch up to her. "You definitely win Most Awkward Entrance."

I glance back at Kamal. His father hands him the airplane and makes soothing noises into his ear, but now that he's started to cry, the little guy doesn't seem able to stop.

Half of business class is glaring at me. If this kid keeps howling, they'll be ready to throw me off the plane before we even leave the ground.

My cheeks fully on fire, I force myself to follow the passenger line into economy. It's already crowded, so the line slows to a stop. I lean around Kiara to see what the holdup is.

Near the back of the plane, Mrs. Sicmaszko, my biology teacher and one of the trip's chaperones, is struggling to lift her carry-on into one of the overhead bins. Her arms tremble with the effort and there's a sheen of sweat on her upper lip.

"Here, I got you, Mrs. S." Wes, the skinniest, palest guy in the senior class, takes her luggage and shoves it into place. He slams the bin shut so hard that I jump. Then he looks up, past me to Spencer and Billy, for a half a beat before he quickly drops back into his seat. The guys make him nervous for good reason. Wes has been one of Spencer's favorite targets since elementary school.

Spencer leans forward. He's the kind of low-grade bully who enjoys striking fear into the hearts of weaker boys more than actually causing them harm. His chest is up against my back and his head looms over mine, making the already cramped space feel even more closed-in. Wes sinks lower in his seat and stares intently at his phone.

The air isn't circulating, so the cabin is stifling. I gather my hair off the back of my neck to cool down, then glance at the passengers to my right. Greendale High seniors take up all the seats in the back of the plane, but there are other people on board, nearly all of them interesting-looking. Red-eye flights are the best for people watching.

Whenever our family flew, Emily would invent stories about the other passengers: where they might be from, what they were planning to do in whatever place they were flying to. She wanted to be a writer and claimed it was good practice—creating characters out of real-world people.

I study a man in an Aerosmith T-shirt that hugs his rounded belly. He's got tattoos covering both of his sizable arms.

He's an accountant who normally wears long sleeves and boring suits to keep his true self secret. But now he's on vacation. Headed to Colorado to join up with his best friends, who are part of a notorious biker gang planning an epic bank heist.

Emily's voice narrates inside my head, nearly as real as if she were whispering these words into my ear. I let out a soft laugh and the Aerosmith guy's gaze flicks to me. He frowns, so I look away quickly and focus my attention on the lady in front of him instead.

She's humming softly to herself, some old-timey tune that sounds like a church hymn. Her gray hair is pulled back neatly from her face and gathered in a loose bun at the nape of her neck. There's a swipe of red lipstick on her razor-thin lips that has migrated to her two front teeth. In her lap is a mound of yarn. She's working a pair of sharp ivory knitting needles through it, forming row after row of stitches. The needles create a *click-clack* rhythm, an underlying beat to her humming.

I try to continue the game, to think of a story for her too, but nothing interesting comes to mind. She's the most ordinary-looking old lady, sitting there in her floral blouse and navy dress pants. She's probably headed to visit her grandkids or something. Or to a church convention. She's definitely got the churchy vibe going with that humming and the prim way she's sitting.

I'm about to move on, choose another passenger to make up a story about, when the old woman looks up. Her eyes lock on mine and a slow smile spreads across her heavily lined face. I start to smile back, but then something in her eyes makes the hairs on the back of my neck stand on end. There's a strange depth to her nearly black irises. If I squint, it's like the blackness shifts and moves. I shiver and she grins wider, showing all her teeth, especially the lipstick-caked ones. The pointy tooth to the right of them is a different color than the others, a weak tea brown that turns my stomach.

I bet she has bad breath.

I glance at Kiara to see if she's noticed the old woman, but Kiara's busy fiddling with her phone, her fingers tapping furiously across the screen.

I turn back to the old woman. She's still watching me with that weird smile, her hands clacking those bone-colored needles together with an almost brutal force, laying down stitch after stitch, her gaze glued on me.

I inhale sharply, and she smiles impossibly wider, her lips stretching taut.

"Well, hello there, dearie," she murmurs softly, her voice musical, if a little creaky. Her eyes widen a bit, and those black irises seem to get bigger, until the whites are nothing but slivers. But then I blink and they're back to normal again.

What was that? I shake my head to try to clear it.

A whisper of cold air caresses my neck. It's totally impossible, but I could swear it's not air at all. It's the old lady's fingers on the base of my skull, playing with my hair. I nearly stumble backward, but then the line starts moving again and I'm propelled forward instead, past the old woman and toward the back of the plane.

"She was weird," I murmur to Kiara.

"Who was?" Kiara continues tapping her phone while she shuffles down the aisle.

"That old lady. Near the front. Super creepy."

"Aren't all old people?" Kiara asks.

I glance over my shoulder, half expecting the lady to be turned around staring at me, but she's not. Only the crown of her silvery head is visible over the top of her seat. I turn around fast. At least she's way up there and I'm all the way back here.

But as I head down the aisle, the *click-clack* of the needles seems to follow me. I can't shake the sound.

Click. Clack.

Click. Clack.

Click. Clack.

Alarms start going off inside my head.

Run. The thought pops into my head unbidden. *Turn around and run.*

But I don't do that anymore, not since Halloween. I touch the locket around my neck. Not since Emily died.

I take out my earbuds and jam them into my ears, then amp up the volume on my phone to a deafening level.

I'm on the plane. I made it this far. I'm not backing out now.

CHAPTER 3

WHEN I GET TO MY SEAT, MY BEST FRIEND, CARTER, IS THERE, NER-
vously pushing his mop of dark curls away from his face.

Crap.

It's not his fault I'm avoiding him. He's done nothing wrong.
It's just that it's too easy to slip back into being my old self around
him. I can't be someone new with the guy who knows me better
than I know myself. Back in September, we signed up for seats
right next to each other. But now I can't imagine sitting beside
him for four hours straight.

I take in his version of ski trip attire: a worn leather jacket
over a black T-shirt and black jeans. He's hunched over a copy of
Entertainment Weekly, working the "I'm an actor" vibe.

"Hey." His flashes an uneasy smile, his posture somehow
hopeful.

I take my earbuds out and pretend to be busy putting them
back in their case.

"You want to take the aisle? 'Cause I'm cool with the middle seat—I mean, I'm just glad you're still sitting with me, 'cause it's been a while since we've talked, so a four-hour plane ride'll give us lots of time." Carter babbles when he's nervous. Right now, his word vomit is out of control, all the words running together.

"Took you long enough, babe. I was getting nervous you'd miss the flight." Kiara's boyfriend, Andrew, waves at her and inches out of the row across from Carter so she can slip past him to the window seat. He gives me a quick nod before he plops back down beside Kiara. She leans in to kiss his cheek.

"Devon, sit with Andrew and me," Kiara says, her forehead still pressed to Andrew's, one hand cupping his cheek.

I can feel Carter waiting to see what I'll decide. Silently pleading for me to choose him.

"Come on, *pleeease*." Kiara whines this last bit dramatically and gestures to the seat next to Andrew, across from Carter. It was supposed to be Emily's. Before October, she and Kiara were the ones who were best friends—ever since fifth grade. Back then, Kiara barely spoke to me. But after Emily died and Kiara volunteered to organize the school's candlelight vigil for her, she glommed on to me and I got absorbed into Emily's friend group. Being with them makes me feel closer to her somehow.

Andrew barely looks up from his journal when I drop down next to him. He's not as friendly as Kiara is. I'm pretty sure I know why. I glance down at my clothes, all of them from Emily's closet. In her clothes and with my dark blond curls ironed straight, I am Emily.

I think it makes him uncomfortable—like he's seeing a ghost. But I want people to see her, not me, to keep her alive however I can. I am to blame for my sister's death as much as the person who hit her. The only way to make up for that is to sacrifice who I was for a version of myself that keeps Emily alive.

"I'd sit beside you, but I need to be able to see outside." Kiara taps the window. "Planes make me claustrophobic."

I put my backpack on the floor and buckle my seat belt.

Suddenly, the seats in front of me bounce violently.

Spencer and Billy plop down next to another guy from the wrestling team. Then Spencer peers back at me, a glint in his eye. "This trip is going to be epic," he says. "Five days in Colorado. Triple-diamond runs. We are gonna tear that mountain up." He winks at me before turning to high-five Billy.

I watch his left leg stretch out into the aisle. A second later, his hand clutches his knee and begins to massage it. It's the one that got injured last winter when someone attacked him at a wrestling meet. It hasn't been right since. He had to sit out his last season because of it.

I doubt with that knee he'll be conquering more than the beginner runs. But Spencer isn't one to admit weakness, even to himself.

"Sir, please place your feet under the seat in front of you," a male flight attendant calls out as he shuts the overhead bins.

"Dude, I'm six-foot-one. My legs don't fit in that little space," Spencer argues.

"I'm sorry, but your legs can't be in the aisle. It's a safety issue." The flight attendant stops near Spencer's seat so he can stare him down.

Grumbling, Spencer finally moves his leg, but he's still got it stretched out enough that his seat leans back, pressing into my knees hard enough to make them ache. Welp, this is gonna be a fun four hours. As soon as we're in the air, I bet he reclines to the maximum. I glance over at my old seat longingly.

"The seat next to me has more room," Carter says, basically reading my mind—or the pained look on my face.

It's going to be damn near impossible to ignore him for the entirety of this flight.

"I just need some space, okay," I blurt, because apparently the old me still controls my mouth sometimes. Emily would've been more tactful. I make a mental note to work on that for next time.

"Oh." Carter's face falls. "I just miss you is all. And if you're mad at me for anything, I'm sorry."

Hearing him apologize even though he's done nothing wrong puts me more on edge. Maybe I should tell him it's like Method acting. He might understand that. If I break character right now and let my Emily-self lapse, I might not be able to get it back.

Someone steps between us and chucks a bag into the overhead bin. It's Yara, one of the coolest girls at Greendale. She glances at me—a quick flick of the eyes.

"You're not sitting over here?" She gestures to my old seat.

I shake my head.

Her eyes settle on my necklace. She gasps.

"What?" I cover my sister's locket with my hand.

She blinks, then shakes her head. "Nothing. It's just I've never seen a locket quite like that one before. It's really pretty. Antique-looking. I like it." She flashes me a quick smile and goes back to staring at her phone.

"I'm in your row. The window seat," she tells Carter as she taps the screen intently.

He stands up so fast his magazine goes careening to the floor. In spite of how determined I am to distance myself from him, I have to stifle a laugh. He's had a crush on this girl ever since freshman year. It's easy to see why. Yara is cover-model beautiful. She always manages to look both like she doesn't try *and* like she curates every outfit carefully. Today, everything she has on is oversized— her hoop earrings, her black square-framed glasses, the camo shirt she wears open with a form-fitting tank top underneath. Even her shoes make a statement: combat boots with a pair of Day of the Dead–style skulls hand-painted on the top of each one.

I stroke Emily's locket. Yara's stamp of approval is a big compliment. Too bad I have no idea where Emily got it.

Yara drops into the window seat and taps Carter's *Entertainment Weekly*. "You read the article in there about the new Jordan Peele movie coming out?"

"Not yet." There's a sudden flush of pink to Carter's cheeks.

"The trailer for it rocks." Yara sighs. "I swear I will do that someday. Mix horror with social commentary like he does, but with a feminist twist."

"Yes, girl," someone a few rows up calls out. Yara raises a fist in the air and smiles.

"That'll be amazing. You know, I'm down to act in any movie you make." Carter leans across the empty seat. "Seriously."

The fact that they're both aiming to work in the movie industry one day either makes them perfect for each other or one hundred percent not. I can't decide. Yara gives Carter a distracted nod as she takes his magazine and starts reading, her whole body leaning toward the window and away from him—given this reaction, it's probably the latter. Oof.

Carter's gaze flicks from her to me and then he hunches over one of his other magazines. Good. Hopefully her not-so-subtle rebuff has him embarrassed enough that he'll leave me alone for a while.

"But my ticket says thirty-four D, see?" Rebecca says too loudly for anyone on the plane to ignore. She's standing in the aisle a few rows up, holding out her phone to the kid currently sitting in that seat so he can see her boarding pass.

Kiara groans. "That girl is always riled up about something."

Rebecca glances in Kiara's direction with her lips pursed.

"I think she heard you," I murmur.

"I hope she did." Kiara stares Rebecca down.

Rebecca makes a face and turns back to the kid in her seat. "Move."

And when he doesn't, she calls for reinforcements.

"Mr. Lewton, he won't move out of my seat." Her voice is ninety percent whine and one hundred percent annoying.

"Fine." The boy moves reluctantly.

"What a witch," Kiara says loudly.

Rebecca gives Kiara the finger.

A bell rings overhead and the flight attendants start securing the cabin for takeoff. I watch the guy attendant check both the bathrooms behind us, then lock them from the outside before he heads to the front of economy to do the safety talk. The plane is maybe only half full. Multiple rows are empty, but despite this, the cabin feels small.

I stare at the misty air rising from the vents above the overhead bins and inhale slowly to soothe the jangling sensation creeping through my nerves, making my heart flutter. With a pilot for a mom, I've flown tons—enough to be over any preflight jitters. But tonight, everything is new and strange because every flight I've taken before has been with Emily.

I cinch my seat belt a little tighter. Then I close my eyes and try to let the hum of the air-circulation system lull me into a state of calm.

All too soon, the engines rev and we roll away from the terminal. Outside, lightning flashes in the distance, far away from the plane, but still.

Kiara leans over Andrew and taps my arm. "Did you see that? Should we be taking off if there's lightning?"

"If the storm were too close, they would've delayed the flight," I say. "Besides, planes are made to withstand lightning strikes. Even if we got hit, we wouldn't crash."

Andrew glances up from his journal at the window. "Can we not talk about this? I used to have nightmares about lightning chasing me as a kid."

I wipe my palms on my jeans. They're all clammy. Between Spencer's stupid plane crash talk on the Jetway, the storm, and Emily not being here, I am massively on edge. I reach up and touch Emily's locket one more time. It's becoming a compulsion.

"That's pretty," Andrew says.

"It was my sister's," I tell him.

"Oh."

He's uncomfortable now. Because I'm mentioning my dead

sister. No one ever knows how to talk to me about her. What the most sensitive thing is to say. I'm not sure I do either.

"Good evening, ladies and gentlemen. Welcome to Flight one-seventy-one from Philadelphia to Denver. My name is Carlos and this is Olivia. . . ." The male flight attendant waves at us from the front of economy as his partner—who's probably only a few years older than me—holds up a seat belt and demonstrates how to use it.

We bump over a rough patch of ground and the plane shudders. Somewhere closer to the front a baby starts to cry. At least it isn't Kamal still freaking out. No one can blame me for setting off *this* baby, not from all the way back here.

I grip my armrests. Suddenly, the crash scene from an old horror movie, *Final Destination,* pops into my head. I try to banish the image of that plane exploding midair, but it lingers in my brain anyway.

"Relax. It'll be a good trip," Andrew murmurs. Kiara grabs his hand and laces her fingers through his. Then she leans her head on his shoulder and winks at me. She's been with Andrew for over two years now. There's an easy familiarity in the way they are around each other. They have the kind of relationship I'd love to have with someone. Once upon a time, I thought that person might be Jack—at least, I'd hoped.

I glance down the aisle at the back of Jack's head, just visible over the top of his seat. I remember running my hands through his hair. The way his lips felt on mine. The way our heartbeats seemed to sync when he held me close. But that was months ago.

The plane makes a wide circle and slowly taxis away from the terminal.

I can't shake this aching unease in the pit of my stomach. As the plane picks up speed, the bad feeling grows. I shouldn't be here. I can't do this. Without Emily, this trip is all wrong.

The lights go off and the plane is plunged into darkness. The engines scream as we hurtle down the runway. I'm pinned to my seat.

Breathe, dummy, I silently tell myself.

I try to ignore the roaring engine, the wailing baby, and the sudden eruption of obnoxious laughter coming from Spencer and his crew, and center myself.

That's when I hear them.

Click-clack, click-clack.

The old lady's knitting needles.

It's impossible. I shouldn't be able to hear them from all the way back here, but somehow, I do. I get a flash of her face in my head, that lipstick-smeared smile and her rotten tooth.

Click-clack.

Click-clack.

The sound feels like an omen. Something's wrong. I shouldn't be on this flight.

Panic makes my insides watery.

I need to get out of here.

Now.

Now.

Now.

But it's too late.

With one final, violent shudder, we lurch into the air and the earth drops away.

CHAPTER 4

THE GROUND GETS FARTHER AND FARTHER AWAY UNTIL IT'S merely a gridwork of lights below us. Lightning flashes to our right. Someone gasps. Then the plane drops all at once, a quick dip that makes my head swim.

"*Aw,* shit!" Billy shouts dramatically.

This makes everyone laugh, including me. It feels good, like someone's released a pressure valve inside me.

A moment later, the plane evens out as we reach cruising altitude. The vibrations stop. There is only the rhythmic roar of the engine and the white-noise sound of air whooshing out of the vents overhead. No knitting-needle *click-clack*s, just muffled conversations between passengers. I release the breath I've been holding.

I was being ridiculous.

Everything's fine.

Outside, the clouds are silvery cotton scattered across the

velvety sky. The lightning is far below us, flashing dully from time to time. Inside the cabin, it's cozy and dim, perfect for napping. Now that the baby has finally settled down, all the passengers are quiet—except for the occasional throat clear or cough. My shoulders relax. I sag into my seat.

In the front galley, Shazia gets up to start organizing the beverage cart. The scent of percolating coffee drifts down the aisle. It's a good smell. Comforting.

The pilot's voice drifts out of the overhead speakers. He blathers on about headwinds and weather reports, his words barely distinguishable over the white noise of the plane's engine. I hear enough to get the gist: conditions are favorable and we're ahead of schedule. We'll be on the ground in just under four hours. He reminds everyone to keep their seat belts fastened even though the flight crew is moving around. Soon we'll get served drinks and those little Biscoff cookies I love.

Mom gets out of her seat and moves into the front galley. She's headed to the crew bunk to catch that nap. Considering her next flight takes off less than two hours after we land, she's going to need it. Her eyes scan the cabin. When she sees me, she waves and I wave back.

"Love you," she mouths, and then ducks out of sight before I can repeat it back.

Most people don't know, but on some planes there's a crew bunk room hidden above business class. Sky Royal has them on all the planes that fly routes four hours or longer. Pilots and flight crew use them to rest. I've always been curious about them, but I've never seen one. I know that the ladder leading up to it is behind one of the front galley cabinets and it can only be unlocked with a flight crew ID.

Thinking about my mom tucked away—alone—sends a pang of worry through me. It's better when she's with people. When she can't spend a lot of time focused on my sister's death. Her grief is always a little bit worse after she's by herself. It's why I was relieved when she went back to work. In those weeks after the funeral, it was like my mom was standing in quicksand, being consumed inch by inch until it seemed inevitable that one day she'd just disappear. I can't lose her too.

Maybe I'll ask Shazia to let me into the bunk room in a bit. Hanging out with my mom would be way better than staying in this seat with my knees squished up. And there are things I want to talk about that would be easier to tackle up there, tucked away from the world.

"Say 'snow bunny.'"

"Snow bunny!"

I glance across the aisle, at the row kitty-corner from mine, in time to see Mai snapping photos of her best friend, Jeanne, with her phone. No doubt she's taking them for Jeanne's social media. Jeanne posts more than ten times per day and has a pretty big following—enough that she's been asked to sponsor some beauty and fashion brands. It's something she brags about to anyone who'll listen. I watch, transfixed as her purple-polished fingers grip the V-neck of her blouse and pull it open so her cleavage shows.

What is it like to be that sure of yourself?

Mai dutifully snaps photo after photo, then lets Jeanne check the images. It's weird because of the two of them, Mai is the stunner, with high cheekbones and these pale green eyes, but Jeanne's always the one who gets all the attention. Still, if it bothers Mai, she never lets on that it does.

Spencer catcalls at the two girls and Jeanne beams, eating up the attention like candy.

The seats in front of me rock as Billy whaps Spencer on the back of the head. "Dude, she's my girlfriend. Knock it off."

"I'm not aiming at her, I'm aiming at Mai, duh," Spencer says back.

Jeanne makes a kissy face at Billy. Mai focuses all her concentration on the phone screen, obviously trying to ignore them.

Because he can't pass up an opportunity to be annoying, Spencer pretends to intercept Jeanne's kiss. Then he and Billy roughhouse until Mr. Lewton yells at them to cut it out.

I lock eyes with Carter out of habit. Normally, we'd trade "Spencer's such an idiot" remarks right about now, but instead I busy myself with retrieving the brochure for Sugar Run Mountain Lodge from my backpack. The place looks pretty stellar. Maybe five days of sun, snow, and skiing will be good for me. The panic that had its claws in me during takeoff fades away completely.

Kiara takes off her scarf, then lowers her tray and sets her laptop on it. While she's waiting for it to power up, she smooths her hair back into a tidy bun.

"We need to start focusing on prom," she tells Andrew as she opens an Excel spreadsheet.

He looks up from his journal. *"Now?"*

"Can you think of a better time?" Kiara's eyes glitter with their usual intensity. "As senior class president, it's my job to make sure this year's event goes off without a hitch—especially after what happened this fall." She clenches her jaw and starts viciously tapping out her password to unlock her laptop. "Five months I've been on probation for something I didn't even do. I would never steal fundraising money. I've never even had detention."

Andrew puts a hand on her shoulder.

"The money was in your locker, babe. I know you didn't put it there—I believe you. But you can see why Principal Riccio and some other people might have their doubts."

Kiara makes an irritated noise.

"It's just not fair. I feel like no matter how hard I try to keep proving myself again and again, there's this shadow of doubt over me. I just want to be free of it . . . and literally wring the neck of whoever put that money in my locker."

"I know," Andrew says gently.

Kiara flicks her eyes up to his and the anger in her face softens slightly.

"I can't stop feeling like the only way to redeem myself is if I plan every aspect of prom down to the last detail. Can you please just support me on this?"

"Yeah, of course." Andrew sets his pen down and closes his journal. He runs one hand over the leather-bound cover wistfully, then tucks it into the seatback pocket. There's a C. S. Lewis quote on the front: "Hardships often prepare ordinary people for an extraordinary destiny."

This is so Andrew. Not even out of high school yet and he's already working to end hunger and provide employment opportunities for the Greendale homeless population. Last year, he created

31

a prototype restaurant that serves them free, high-quality meals while also setting them up with job interviews conducted during those meals. It's been so successful that other restaurants are being planned in four more communities in our state. Andrew's even been on the local morning show to talk about it. Prom is nothing more than a silly distraction to him. The fact that he's helping Kiara anyway is a testament to how much he loves her. If he and Kiara stay together, she'll rule the world and he'll try to save it.

"We need to go over the list of approved photographers Mr. Lewton gave us and pick one," Kiara says. "I downloaded their work portfolios last night. And Devon, I'd like you to weigh in too, since you're officially on the committee now." She angles her laptop so Andrew and I can both see.

I sigh.

If I'd known she wanted me to sit here so I could go over prom photographers with her, I'd have kept my original seat. The case file I've been building for Emily's hit-and-run is in my backpack. I was planning on going over it again. There could be some detail I'm overlooking that might lead me in the right direction.

But then Emily's face floats through my brain.

If she were here, she'd be helping. It's her spot on the committee that I took over. Emily loved this sort of stuff. It's why she and Kiara were so close. They both shared the overachiever gene. Not me. I would rather squirt lemon juice into my eye than sort through photographer portfolios. Why can't she have me research bands? That's something I could get into.

I tap out a series of beats against my thighs and for a second let myself miss all those Saturday nights spent playing, my hair so wet with sweat it stuck to my cheeks, the crowd dancing wildly just beyond the stage, everyone drenched in neon light. Music drowning out everything and everyone.

"Devon? Focus," Kiara orders.

I try, but despite my best efforts, it only takes a few minutes of debating the advantages of balloon arches versus no balloon arches before my mind starts to wander again.

That's when the old woman captures my attention. She's in the aisle and headed this way.

Her gnarled fingers grip the sides of the seats as she passes row after row. The knitting needles, still clutched in her left hand, *click-clack* against the hard seatbacks. She's humming, loud enough to get people's attention as she passes. But she doesn't seem to notice them because she's staring at me again.

Not in my general direction.

Right. At. Me.

There is a yellowing stain on the collar of her blouse and her pants are bunched up, so her swollen, nylon-encased ankles show. The scent of mothballs wafts down the aisle.

Worms of anxiety wriggle inside my stomach. It's ridiculous. She's just a little old lady who's probably headed to the bathroom.

But to get there, she's going to have to pass our row.

When I think about her hand on my seat, those twisted, fat-knuckled fingers that close to me, dread coils through my insides. I can't explain why. It's got something to do with that stupid grin of hers and the way her pupils look too wide for her eyes. Or maybe she reminds me of a character in this Stephen King short story Emily forced me to read last summer when her inexplicable obsession with horror novels started. Yeah, that's it, she's like the bedridden grandma in that story.

Some old people are straight-up creepy. I think maybe it's because, with all their maladies, they're walking billboards for death, glaring reminders of how it's eating away at all of us with its sharp teeth, one nibble at a time, then in giant, ghastly gulps.

She inches forward, her thick-soled sensible black flats shuffling over the floor.

Shoosh.

Shoosh.

Get a hold of yourself, Devon.

I try to shake the disquiet making me want to fidget or flee.

Shoosh.

Shoosh.

She's more than halfway to our row, her gaze still firmly focused on me. I glance at Andrew and Kiara to see if they've noticed, but they're completely absorbed with Kiara's spreadsheet. And Carter is leaning over the *Entertainment Weekly* spread out on the empty seat between Yara and him.

Rebecca is reading a book. Wes is unwrapping a candy bar. Spencer and Billy are totally preoccupied watching some movie on Billy's laptop. Mai is braiding Jeanne's hair. Jack's facing forward. No one seems to be aware that the old lady is in the aisle, much less grinning at me like she's about to unhinge her mouth and swallow me whole.

Okay, you're losing it, Devon. She's just somebody's grandmother.

"Ma'am, the captain hasn't turned off the seat belt sign yet. Please return to your seat." The flight attendant who did the safety talk before we took off—Carlos, I think he said his name was—intercepts the old lady a mere three rows away from mine.

"But I have to use the ladies'." The old woman's voice is timid, almost musical with the slightest hint of a Southern accent that makes me think she's not originally from Philadelphia like we are.

"I'm sorry, ma'am. But until the captain turns off the seat belt sign, you'll have to remain in your seat for your own safety. It should only be a few more minutes."

"But *you're* up."

"Yes. I'm on the flight crew."

The old lady leans around Carlos and peers down the aisle. Her smile turns into a frown. "I'm going to the ladies' right now, young man. Waiting at my age isn't an option."

Carlos looks momentarily flummoxed, but when she tries to get around him, he puts his arm out to block her. "Ma'am. No. If there's turbulence and you were to fall . . ."

The old lady waves dismissively.

"I'm not going to fall."

She tries to go around him again, this time pushing into him to make him move.

"I said no." Carlos braces his feet and holds his ground.

The old lady eyes him calmly. Then suddenly, that weird grin slowly spreads across her face again. By now, most of the plane has noticed the standoff. The air grows still, tense. Several passengers have their phones up so they can record whatever's about to go down. Of course aspiring horror movie director Yara is among them. She holds her phone over her head so she can get a clear angle.

"Let me by or I will tell everyone on this plane your secret." The old woman's voice has lost its lilt.

Carlos folds his arms. "Ma'am, go back to your seat. How about if I bring you some coffee while you wait for the light to go off, okay? Or tea, maybe?" He eyes Olivia, the other flight attendant, and she heads for the business class galley, probably to get the coffee.

"I'll tell them about those girls. All those bars. And the little pills." The old lady shakes her knitting needles in front of Carlos's face like a pair of wagging, disapproving fingers.

Carlos recoils. "Excuse me?"

"Can't charm them without a little help, can you? Much too dull for that." She looks pointedly at the black silicone wedding band on Carlos's left hand. "What would your wife say if she knew what you were up to?"

Carlos's hands ball into fists at his side.

I gasp. What she's accusing him of is awful. But even worse is the guilty look he's too caught off guard to hide. I don't know how she could possibly know what she knows, but somehow, she does. I gape at Carlos, at his soft, pudgy body. He looks like half the middle-aged men I see around Greendale. I would've never suspected him of being a sexual predator like she's suggesting.

Carlos grabs hold of her arm so hard his knuckles turn white. "You're going back to your seat right now."

"Carlos?" Shazia rushes toward him and the old lady.

When he turns to Shazia to explain the situation, the old lady wrenches free of his grip and babbles a bunch of incoherent syllables. It's gibberish. The old lady's really losing it. Is she having

36

a stroke? But no . . . there is something rhythmic about them, something distinctly ordered. Like an ancient language.

Suddenly, the old lady jerks the knitting needles above her head with the sharp ends of both pointing down.

Before I can make sense of what's happening, she plunges them into Carlos's chest.

CHAPTER 5

CARLOS SHRIEKS BEFORE STUMBLING BACKWARD INTO THE other flight attendant.

I let out a scream.

The old lady yanks the needles out of Carlos. There's this horrible sucking sound when they break loose. How can knitting needles do that? Puncture a man's chest like that?

Shazia stumbles, falls into one of the empty seats in the row beside her.

I unbuckle my seat belt before I'm even aware I'm doing it.

What if the old lady goes after her too?

"Someone stop her!" several people yell, nearly in unison. The airplane fills with screams as more and more people realize what's happening.

I step out into the aisle as the old lady stabs Carlos again. And again. Each thrust is more forceful than the last. It's wet, the sound of the needles puncturing Carlos's chest now. Blood sprays in a wet arc, speckles the old lady's face. Her tongue darts out and tastes a droplet that lands on her lips.

My mouth goes dry. I can't make my arms and legs move. I'm completely frozen in place. But my insides are roiling. Oh, God, I might throw up. All that blood and the way she tasted it. I swallow down bile.

What do I do?

What would my sister do?

I want to be brave enough to tackle the old woman, get her away from Carlos and Shazia . . . but those needles. The thought of them stabbing into my own chest has my lungs tightening. I am a statue, motionless, unable to do anything but watch this nightmare playing out in front of me.

"Oh my God!" Kamal's dad is out of his seat with the little boy, inching backward, his gaze never leaving the old lady as he makes his way to the front of the plane, as far from her as he can manage. He clutches Kamal tighter to his chest.

Spencer and Billy bolt out of their seats. From the other side of the plane, Jack climbs over the people in his row to get into the aisle so he can sneak up behind the old woman. He's too close, within stabbing distance.

As much as I've cursed him over the past few months, in this moment, all I feel is horror. I want to yell at him to get away from her. Run. But if I do, I'll give away his position to the old woman.

I manage a step forward. If I can keep her distracted, give her a reason to look this way so she doesn't notice Jack . . .

"Devon, don't." Andrew grabs my arm.

The old lady pulls her needles from Carlos's chest one last time. Carlos staggers forward, into Shazia, who has managed to get back on her feet. Shazia drags him out of range of the old woman as Spencer and the other boys hem the old lady in. Jack has his arms out like he's ready to grab her from behind. Olivia returns from business class and closes ranks next to him. She's holding up a set of plastic cuffs instead of the coffee she went up there for. Her hands are visibly shaking.

The old lady stands in the aisle a moment, needles raised over her head again. She studies the people in the seats closest to her. They shrink as far away from her as they can. She jabs the needles at them almost playfully, seems to relish the fresh round of screams that erupt. Then the old woman presses both needles to her mouth. Her lips move wordlessly against them. She's muttering something, too low to be heard. But the way her mouth moves . . . it looks as if she's speaking more nonsensical syllables like before. Are they some kind of prayer . . . or a curse?

Adrenaline courses through my veins. Is she going to stab one of the boys now? I wrench free of Andrew's grip. If I'm going to cause a distraction, now's the time.

The old lady locks eyes with me. She raises one eyebrow as if she's amused—as if *I* amuse her—and then holds out her hands and lets the needles drop. They clatter to the ground and bounce over the carpet—once, twice, before rolling to a stop at my feet. Why did she drop them when she saw me standing here?

Her eyes still bore into mine. I swear it's like I can feel her— some intangible part of her—clawing at my brain again, trying to pry it open and see inside. The hairs on my arms and the back of my neck stand up.

She isn't human.

The thought reverberates through my head.

I grip the seatback beside me. Suddenly, the locket around my neck grows cold enough to send goose bumps down my arms.

I can't explain it, but it was Emily's voice I just heard, not my own. Her words clear as anything—like she physically whispered them into my ear.

My legs betray me and go weak. I stagger backward, collapse into my seat. Hunching down low, I use the seatback in front of me to hide from the old woman's view. The ivory-hued needles are there on the ground, gleaming softly in the dark space by my feet. I can't seem to take my eyes off them. They are nearly the same size and shape as a pair of my drumsticks.

Wait . . . are they *glowing*?

While I watch, the blood coating them slowly disappears as if it's sucked into the needles themselves. Symbols flare into existence, scroll bloody red across the length of each needle before they vanish nearly as fast as they appeared.

My goose bumps keep spreading until they cover my entire body. There is something electric in the air, invisible, but undeniably present and constant, like the hum of the airplane's engines.

"Boys, let the attendants deal with her," Mr. Lewton cautions Spencer, Billy, and Jack, but it's too late. The moment they realize the needles are on the carpet, they swoop in on the old woman.

I lean into the aisle as Jack throws his arms around the old lady's waist and Spencer knocks her feet out from under her. I pick up the knitting needles to get them out of the old lady's reach. They feel alive. Energy vibrates through them like they're tuning forks.

The sound of the old lady hitting the floor is bone-crushingly loud. Her breath rushes out in one noisy whoosh. It's stale and there's this tang of something rotten beneath it—that tooth. I hold my nose to keep from smelling it.

The old lady is sprawled on the carpet.

She looks up at me, that awful smile still plastered onto her blood-speckled face.

"It begins," she whispers.

CHAPTER 6

"AIR MARSHAL. LET ME THROUGH." A MAN WHO LOOKS MORE like a suburban dad than an air policeman in his jeans-and-button-down-shirt combo strides briskly to where the boys have the old lady pinned. "Hands out in front of you," he orders the old woman.

"Olivia, the cuffs, please." The air marshal gives the flight attendant a brief, reassuring smile.

She hands him the set of plasti-cuffs. He crouches beside the old woman and his jacket opens enough for me to see a gun holstered under his right arm. He doesn't reach for it because the old lady willingly offers up her wrists to be cuffed. Once she's restrained, Spencer and Jack help haul her to her feet. The plane is alive with wide-eyed chatter.

"Is there a doctor on board?" Shazia asks as she maneuvers Carlos toward the back galley, applying pressure to his wounds. "Or any other medical personnel?"

"I'm okay," Carlos says, but there's a dazed look in his eyes. He's covered in so much blood.

"No, you're not. You're going into shock," Shazia murmurs, eyeing his gray-tinged skin.

"I'm a doctor." A woman hurries down the aisle.

She helps Shazia lay Carlos on the galley floor. There's blood trickling out of his mouth now too. I've watched enough *Grey's Anatomy* episodes to know this isn't good. He's bleeding internally. His hands twitch reflexively at his side. Shazia's right: he *is* going into shock. The carpet beneath him is wet and glistening with his blood. Kneeling beside him, the doctor begins to gently examine the wounds to his neck and chest.

I put a hand to my own chest, feel the pounding of my heart through my shirt. The last few minutes have been like something out of a movie, violent and surreal. I'm half nauseous from nerves, my whole body humming. I feel like I've been electrocuted or something. What is *happening*? I can't make sense of any of it. All that business about Carlos and his secrets and these knitting needles. I stare down at them. The strange script is gone and so is the blood. I can't keep from shuddering. These things probably mortally wounded that flight attendant, which means they are potential murder weapons.

"If everyone will remain in their seats, please," the air marshal orders as he begins to pat the old woman down, looking for more weapons, I guess. When he seems satisfied there aren't any, he hauls her to her feet. That unsettling grin of hers doesn't falter the entire time. There's blood peppered all over her face and chest, bright red dots that match her lipstick. But she doesn't seem to care. She winks at a kid seated to her left. Even from where I'm sitting, I can hear him gasp.

Shazia clears her throat. "The seat belt sign is still on, so those passengers in the aisle should return to their seats." She's trying to sound in control, but there's no mistaking the tremor in her voice.

Jack and Billy stagger back to their rows, frowning like they're disappointed, like they've been cheated out of a fight. Only Spencer remains in the aisle, his body still wired for action.

"Sit down," Shazia orders.

Spencer glares down at the old lady for a long second, his chest puffed out. Then he rolls his shoulders and, limping slightly, heads back to his seat. When he passes Mai, he tips his head at her like some heroic cowboy in an old Western movie.

"That should earn me a date in the hot tub tomorrow," he whispers to Billy as he drops into his seat.

I kick his seatback. "Dude, a guy just got stabbed. Have a little respect."

"Jealous?" Spencer grins at me from around the back of his chair.

"Definitely not." I glare at him.

The air marshal leads the old woman toward the last row of seats where he was sitting alone before all hell broke loose. She's humming again, the same song from when I passed her during boarding, loud enough so everyone can hear this time.

Carlos makes a low groaning sound in response. Shazia presses a towel to his wounds while the doctor unzips the black bag full of medical supplies Olivia brought her and begins hurriedly going through the contents. Olivia paces in the corner of the galley, her hands pressed to her mouth, her eyes shiny with tears.

"You're going to be okay, hang in there." She murmurs it over and over, and I'm not sure if she's talking to Carlos or herself or both.

The old lady hums even louder. When I turn around, she's staring at me again.

"What the actual eff," Kiara whispers, her gaze moving between me and the woman.

"Young Devon." The blood is still wet and shiny on the old lady's face when she calls to me. So much blood. On her. Leaking out of Carlos. The coppery smell sends a fizz of revulsion through me. I inch closer to Andrew, and he places one arm across me protectively. I can feel him trembling.

"How do you know my name?" I ask. Blood rushes into my head, making my temples throb. I slide the knitting needles under my leg, out of sight. I don't want her to know I have them.

"It's awful. What happened to your Emily. Bad enough when a regular sister dies—but a twin? It's like losing a limb, isn't it? Like you died in a way too. Do you still feel her?" She eyes my clothes. "You're becoming her. Do you want to take her place? Under the ground? In the dark?"

"Leave her the hell alone." Carter is out of his seat and glaring at the woman.

"How do you know about Emily?" I ask loudly enough to be heard over Carter. My voice is hoarse, scraped raw by emotion.

Her eyes bore into mine and I feel her mentally probing my insides again. It's like bugs crawling under my skin.

"I see you've decided to push your way into her friend group too." She eyes Kiara and Andrew. He shudders and sinks deeper into his seat. "Do they sometimes call you by her name by accident? I bet that gives you a thrill. That for one second you aren't yourself. Especially after what you did."

"Screw you," I say through gritted teeth. Anger burns white-hot through my core. I don't know how she knows what she knows, but everyone is staring at me. I'm exposed, laid bare. It's almost too much to take. I bite my bottom lip so hard I draw blood.

The old lady lets out a soft, girlish giggle. "Oh, this is going to be so much fun."

The air marshal growls at her to be quiet.

"What is wrong with her?" Andrew moves his arm off me and cranes his head so he can look at the old bat.

"Dementia, maybe?" Kiara gazes out the window at the endless dark beyond. "Dementia patients get mean and violent sometimes."

On the surface this seems plausible . . . except how does the old woman know all these things? About Carlos. About Emily. About me. I wrap my arms around myself. Now *I'm* the one trembling.

Shazia picks up the phone on the wall beside the jump seat in the back galley. She speaks into it, makes a face, hangs up, and tries again. Then she hurries up the aisle to the cockpit door and raps on it several times.

She must be informing the pilots of the situation. Good. We'll have to divert to the nearest airport now so Carlos can get the medical attention he needs, and they can haul that psycho witch off the plane. Pretty soon, this whole weird flight will be over, and we'll be on the ground. Safe. It can't happen fast enough.

Shazia hurries to the back galley again. She and Olivia huddle together. I look up at the speakers above my head. When is the pilot going to come on and tell us which airport we'll be landing at?

"I don't like this." Andrew stares intently at the flight attendants. "Why do they look so freaked out?"

I strain my ears trying to hear what they're saying, but I only manage to catch snippets.

"Called twice."

"No."

"No one did."

"We're cut off."

"Are they talking about the pilots? Or air traffic control, maybe?" I ask out loud. What does that mean? Cut off? Was the old woman a distraction for someone else, a terrorist or something? A dozen possible explanations for why we might not have contact with the cockpit or air traffic control run through my head. None of them are good. I study the ceiling. Is my mom okay in the crew bunk? Could people have been hiding up there? Used her to gain access to the cockpit while the rest of us were focused on the old lady? I want to go to her and make sure she's safe, but I'm not allowed to leave my seat right now.

Carter shrugs helplessly. "I can't tell. Maybe."

"Um, excuse me. What is happening?" Yara asks, half standing in her seat. She has her phone angled at the galley.

The flight attendants glance back at us, concerned expressions plastered on all their faces.

Before they can say anything, the old lady clears her throat. "I suppose it's time I explain what's really going on here, children. But first, we'll need a smidge of privacy." Her voice is clear and high and laced with a singsong quality, a caricature of a grandma voice. It's not the voice she used with me or with Carlos.

"Be quiet," the air marshal orders her a second time, but she ignores him. Sitting up straight, she draws in a rattling breath that seems to go on longer than is humanly possible, then holds it in for a count of three. Her mouth opens wide, wide, wide, and a grayish smoke pours out from somewhere deep in her throat. So much smoke. Too much to be coming out of one old woman. It creeps over the row in front of her and spills into the aisle like zombie movie fog.

Dread snakes through me. What is that? Some kind of poison? It can't be good, whatever it is.

"Don't breathe it in! Hurry. Get your oxygen masks on!" I yell so every passenger can hear, but the fog expands and thickens fast, obscuring the floor, the seats, everything in its path.

I claw at the ceiling where the oxygen masks are supposed to drop from in case of an emergency landing, but I can't seem to find the release button.

Kiara and Andrew are trying too. But it's too late. The fog is already all around us. Thick and blinding. I clap a hand over my nose and mouth. I can't see. But I can hear.

Over and over come the dull sounds of bodies dropping heavily to the floor.

CHAPTER 7

THE FOG HANGS IN THE AIR FOR WHAT FEELS LIKE AN ETERNITY. I hold my breath until my lungs scream in protest, until little black dots pepper my vision. Then my body turns traitor and forces me to suck in air. I wait for the fog to poison me, for my body to drop to the floor like the other passengers.

Except I don't.

I take another cautious breath.

Then two more.

Next to me, Andrew is panting hard, and Kiara is talking to herself.

"We're okay. We're going to be okay," she says, her voice commanding, not reassuring—as if through sheer force of will she'll make this true.

"Devon?" Carter's voice cuts through the fog. His hand appears, searching for mine.

"I'm here."

His voice steadies me. I reach out and grab his hand. I need to feel the solidness of my best friend because this moment has the strangeness of a dream—no, a nightmare—and I need to hold on to something—someone—real.

Little by little the fog starts to dissipate.

Soon, I can see the outlines of the other people. All the Greendale kids have spilled out into the aisles. Rebecca is clinging tightly to Wes. Normally she barely acknowledges he exists, but now she's holding on to him for dear life. Other kids are just standing there with shell-shocked expressions on their faces. But the adults . . . they're all still seated, unmoving. Unconscious—oh, God—or worse.

"Hey, they're not responding," Jack calls from his seat near the middle of the plane.

"Who?" Kiara stands up, cranes her head to see.

"Mrs. Sicmaszko, Mr. Lewton. They're just, I don't know, knocked out." He holds up one of Mrs. Sicmaszko's arms and lets it drop limply back into her lap for emphasis.

"But they have a pulse, right?" I ask.

Jack blinks at me. This is the first time I've talked to him since the day I accused him of murdering Emily. The weight of his gaze sends a tremor through me. I press my lips into a firm line. Just because I'm asking him a question doesn't mean I've cleared him off my suspect list the way the police have from theirs.

Or that those feelings mean anything.

"Uh, yeah. Her pulse is strong," Jack says, his voice slightly hoarse the way it gets when he's stressed.

"The little kids are out cold too." Mai points at Kamal. He's collapsed in his father's arms, head lolling, mouth open, a thin line of drool hanging from his bottom lip. It's unsettling enough that the adults are out, but the little kids? I look away from Kamal because I have this sudden, overwhelming urge to cry.

Why? Why all of them and not us?

I shift in my seat. Is the old woman unconscious? But the moment I think it, I know she's not. The fog came from her.

Sure enough, the old woman is awake—alert as ever—though thankfully still buckled into the seat beside the air marshal. Her cuffed hands rest peacefully in her lap. In the galley behind her, the entire flight crew, as well as the doctor, is sprawled across the floor.

I have to get to my mom. Find out if she's okay. I rush to Shazia's side. I need her ID card to get to the bunk room. She's lying half in and half out of the galley. Carefully, I move her so she's on her back. Her hijab shifts so a sliver of her black hair shows. As gently as I can I push it back into place. Her skin is warm when I feel her wrist for a pulse. The vein under my finger thumps steadily; her heartbeat is strong, just like Mrs. Sicmaszko's and Mr. Lewton's. I let out a whoosh of air. She's okay.

"Oh, they're all very much alive," the old lady says pleasantly, as if she's talking to me about the weather. "I merely put them into a temporary hibernation. The littlest ones too. Given how much that baby hollered during takeoff, you should thank me."

"Why are you doing this?" Spencer looms over her seat row, his chest heaving. But he doesn't dare to get any closer or touch her this time. The boldness he had before is gone. His hands are trembling at his sides.

"Because they aren't part of the game we're playing." The old lady crosses her legs demurely and tucks them under her seat.

While she's focused on Spencer, I slip Shazia's lanyard over her head and quickly tuck it into the pocket of my sweater.

Spencer makes an exasperated noise. "We're not playing any game."

"Oh, but you are. The moment you stepped on this plane. And it won't end until I get what I need."

"What is the game?" I ask softly, my heart hammering inside my chest. Am I dreaming? I pinch the inside of my arm, but nothing changes. This, whatever it is, is real.

When the old lady's blue-black eyes focus on me again, the unbridled glee in them is palpable. She licks her cracked, bloodsplattered lips. "It's a mystery game. Like Clue. The point is to discover who is the most deserving."

Kiara steps out into the aisle. "Most deserving? Of what?" She's wrapped her scarf protectively around her arms like it's a suit of armor.

The old woman's laugh is a hoard of rats running over my skin, equal parts repulsive and unsettling.

"Of sacrificing, of course," she says.

"Stop talking nonsense!" I yell loud enough to make my temples throb. She seems to be drawing the moment out on purpose, relishing it. The old me and all her hotheaded impulsiveness is slipping through the Emily veneer I've built. I'm losing my composure.

The old woman raises an eyebrow and smirks. Unlike me, she's fully in control. I place my hands flat on the floor to steady myself. I feel light-headed, like I might pass out.

"Go on," Spencer says. His hands close into fists.

"I am in need of a new host body." She tilts her head and glances down at herself. "This one is nearly worn out." Pausing dramatically, the old lady gazes at each of us and her eyebrow arches. "So I will be taking one of yours. Once the rest of you choose who it will be."

Mai lets out a hysterical burst of laughter. "What? This makes zero sense. She's certifiably insane."

More and more kids have crowded around us to listen. All of them start chattering at once.

"What is she talking about?"

"She wants us to choose a host body? What does that mean? Like, to possess?"

"This has to be a joke."

"I assure you it is not," the old woman says. "I have inhabited this body since nineteen forty-eight, but now it is failing. In order to live on, I must find a new one."

"She believes she's, like, what? A demon?" This question comes from Rebecca. She's frowning at the old woman. Her hand goes up to touch the tiny gold crucifix around her neck.

"You think we're on one of those prank shows? Like on TruTV or Netflix or something?" Billy asks. He studies the ceiling of the plane and starts to laugh nervously. "Okay, so where're the hidden cameras at?"

"I already told you this is not a joke." The old lady makes a growling, inhuman sound that reverberates through the whole plane, into my chest, into the deepest part of me. I glance around.

Judging from the expressions on everyone else's faces, it's affecting them the same way.

What she's saying . . . Rebecca is on the right track. It's like something out of a horror movie. *Evil.*

Could she really be something not quite human?

I remember those words spoken in Emily's voice inside my head earlier.

"Are you a demon?" I ask.

The old lady cocks her head. "No. I am an immortal being without an immortal body, so I must possess other bodies in order to survive. Every creature has its limitations, even me. However, what I am is not nearly as important as what I *need.* Because giving it to me is the only way you and your friends will make it off this plane alive."

I stand up.

"Tell us what we have to do. What are the rules of your game?" I try to sound calmer than I feel, but inside I am frantic.

"The only rule is that a decision must be made, and you and your classmates must make it. Choose one of you for me to possess. Who you pick doesn't matter. How you decide doesn't matter. Only that you do." She smacks her lips. "Oh, and there is a time limit. You must choose before this flight is over."

"And if we don't? Choose?" Andrew peers at her from over his seatback. "Then what?"

The old woman's watery blue eyes lose their good humor and turn flinty.

"You die."

CHAPTER 8

ONE MINUTE I'M IN THE GALLEY STARING AT THE OLD LADY, THE next I'm buckled into my seat again, the old lady's knitting needles jamming into my thighs. I clutch Shazia's ID card tightly. Whatever's happening is too big for me to handle—for any of us to handle. I need my mom. I try to unbuckle, but I can't. The latch won't budge.

"What's going on?" Kiara's voice is shrill with fear. "We were all out in the aisle and now . . ."

"Devon?" Carter grips his seat arms so hard his knuckles go white. "How did we end up back at our seats?"

I twist around. The old woman is still buckled into the back row, but her eyes are closed. She's murmuring those nonsense-sounding syllables again. Inside my jeans pocket, the knitting needles seem to grow warmer.

Suddenly, the plane goes dark. Only the emergency lights are on, bathing the cabin in a weird, reddish glow. The engines cut off. The constant humming noises disappear. The plane rocks left then right. Shudders. Drops.

We start to free-fall.

I scream as my whole body goes weightless. The only thing keeping me from crashing into the ceiling is my seat belt.

The flight crew's unconscious bodies rise into the air and slam into the ceiling, then hurl past my head, limp human projectiles as the plane plummets down, down, down. Shazia's head hits the partition separating business class from economy with a bone-shattering crack that makes one of her eyes pop out of its socket. Safety masks drop out of the ceiling. The seat belt signs illuminate all over the plane. Alarms blare.

"Make it stop!" Rebecca shrieks.

Screams fill the air.

I look out the window. Clouds rush past. Soon I spot a sprinkling of lights below. Land.

We're falling so fast. My stomach is in my mouth. Bile rushes up my throat.

The plane vibrates violently. And then the midplane emergency doors fly off. Wind whips through the cabin as it depressurizes. My ears fill with the sound of rushing air. The overhead bins burst open. Baggage tumbles out and slams into people, the walls, the floor. Carter narrowly avoids being hit by a laptop. Rivets meant to hold the ceiling of the plane in place begin machine-gunning through the air.

Mom is up there. Alone.

A carry-on hits Yara in the head. Her screams die in her throat as blood explodes out of her skull. Clothing and newspapers and books whirl past. Shazia's body and the bodies of the other flight attendants get ripped out the exits. Then several rows of unconscious passengers, including Kamal and his dad. The roof peels back near the front of the plane, where the crew bunk is.

"Mom!" I shout. My voice is swallowed up in the chaos. Judging from the gaping hole above me, there's no way she's still on the plane. She's gone.

The plane groans loudly.

I watch, horrified, as Rebecca reaches for something, anything, to hold on to as the row she's in gets yanked from its place and hurled out of the plane. The wind is so loud. I can't hear my own screams. I can't think. I can only feel the inexorable pressure, pulling at me, wrenching my seat from the floor.

A few seconds more and we're all dead.

"Oh, God, make it stop!" I yell into the air. "Please, make it stop." My face is wet with tears. I repeat the same plea over and over until I'm hoarse.

Andrew, Kiara, Carter, and Spencer join in. Then Jack, Wes, Billy, Mai, and Jeanne. Pretty soon, every Greendale kid left on the plane is chanting, begging. "Please. Stop. MAKE IT STOP!"

But we're still falling and falling.

I can see buildings now. Houses and roads and cars. We are going to die.

I throw my hands up and brace for impact and scream until my vocal cords are scraped raw.

Then suddenly, as fast as it all went chaotic, everything goes utterly and completely still. Silent.

I open my eyes, tears streaming down my face. My heart

aches from beating so fast. My lungs are tight from lack of oxygen and my throat feels shredded. I clutch my chest and try to breathe.

The lights snap on.

The hum of circulating air and engine noise resumes.

The plane is back at cruising altitude, and I'm in the galley next to Shazia again. She's back, but still unconscious. The whole flight crew is. And Rebecca. Kamal and his dad. The engines rumble beneath my feet. The overhead compartments are shut tight. The emergency exits are in place. The roof is intact. Every row of passengers is where it should be.

None of what just happened was real.

"Now you know what I'm capable of," the old woman says.

I inhale sharply.

Her face has changed. It's the wrinkles around her eyes and mouth. They've deepened, and her lips are ringed with lines, the lipstick bleeding into each one until her mouth looks like it has red stitches around it. She nods at the TV screens in the back of each seat. A digital countdown clock appears on all of them: 3:00:20, 3:00:19, 3:00:18. "You have just over three hours left. Use them wisely. Choose your sacrifice."

Carter and Yara—who is once again completely unharmed—gasp in unison.

The tips of my fingers and toes go numb. I turn to face the old lady, my mouth dry, my entire body filled with dread. Everyone is watching me, wide-eyed.

"What happens to the person you possess?" I ask. "I mean, to their soul?"

"I absorb them. They live inside me, but they cannot take control of their body."

"So, basically, they're trapped. For how long?"

The old woman shakes her head. "Forever. Their souls travel with me to the next body and the next and the next."

Everything in me recoils. What she's describing sounds like hell. Like eternal torment.

"How could we sentence someone to that?" I ask.

I feel the weight of her stare on my back. "Because otherwise you will die. Every single person on this plane. But if you dislike the idea of choosing someone so much, I could also accept a volunteer. I would happily take you, for instance." Her eyes light up. The black in her pupils spreads, suffocates what little blue they contained. "Then you could really atone for your sins. Be the hero."

Her words both scare me and stir something in me.

Don't!

Emily's voice shouts inside my head. So loud I press my hands to my ears.

The old lady frowns as she studies me.

I shake my head to clear it.

What was that?

Still frowning, the old lady flicks her gaze from me to the others.

"Then maybe you? Or you?"

She points a gnarled finger at Billy and then Wes.

"Any reason you boys might be tempted to give up your lives? Any unforgivable sins?" There is something knowing in her expression. She sees all of us more clearly than we can see each other, or ourselves, and this is maybe the most terrifying thing about her.

Both boys instinctively back away.

She looks in Jack's direction, but Jack looks at me instead of her. There is a question in his gaze.

Would I want him to be the sacrifice?

If he killed my sister, yes. But I still don't have the proof I need to know for sure.

He flinches, as if he can discern my thoughts.

"Or you?" The old lady raises an eyebrow at Rebecca, who avoids her gaze.

"Ah, how utterly unsurprising." She practically giggles. "None of you willing to save everyone else if it means sacrificing yourself. So many deserving candidates," the old lady says, her voice growing serious, her eyes flashing. "Some more than others. It will be fascinating to see who you choose."

But how can we possibly decide something as awful as this?

As if reading my mind, the old lady smiles. "Don't worry. When the time is right and all of your secrets have been laid bare, you will."

HOUR TWO

CHAPTER 9

"I DON'T WANNA DIE!" A GIRL HOLLERS LIKE HER SOUL IS BEING torn in two.

"This is not happening." Wes paces the aisle before he drops down next to Mr. Lewton. "Wake up. Come on, please." His eyes get shiny as he tries unsuccessfully to rouse the man.

I've never seen any of my classmates like this. I should do something, but what? Panic snakes its way through me, squeezes my heart in a death grip.

"Help us," Jeanne says like somehow someone will just poof into existence, wave a magic wand, and make the events of the last half hour disappear.

"What about the pilots?" I ask myself more than anyone else. I'm desperate to focus on anything other than the hysteria building inside me. "They have to be awake, right?"

"True," Spencer says. "How else is the plane still in the air?" He and Billy struggle out of their seats and haul ass to the front of the plane. Rebecca and several others follow, as if the sudden explosion of forward motion snaps them out of their panicked stupors. Yara records them running up the aisle, her eyes wide.

I want to follow, but I'm paralyzed by panic. I look back at the old woman.

Her gaze flits from one hysterical kid to the next, her tongue darting out between her lips as if she can taste our fear in the air.

Across the aisle, a boy wedges himself into the narrow footwell between seat rows, out of sight.

Boom!

Spencer slams into the cockpit door with the full weight of his massive body.

Boom!

He hurls himself again and again and again.

Billy grabs the flight crew phone off the wall.

"Hello? Can anyone hear me?" he yells.

The old lady giggles.

Jeanne starts shaking random passengers.

"Wake up!" she screams into one guy's face as she tugs him nearly out of his seat. He is limp, head lolling. "COME ON, you stupid jerk!" She slaps him. The sound is gunshot-loud.

Mai pulls at her shoulder. "That's enough."

Jeanne bends over, chest heaving.

"I can't do this. I can't, I can't, I can't," she says over and over.

"No one's responding." Spencer rams into the cockpit door one more time, hard enough that his injured knee buckles. Billy grabs his friend's arm to steady him.

Rebecca stares down the aisle, her eyes glazed, unseeing.

Help them.

My sister's voice echoes through my head again, clear enough to jolt me out of my panic. I take a breath, put two fingers in my mouth, and whistle as loudly as I can.

The sound is shrill enough to startle everyone into silence.

"We need to calm down. Think about what to do," I say.

"She's right," Jack says. He's beside the kid crammed into the footwell. "Back to your seats, everyone."

Spencer rubs his sore knee and glares at the cockpit door one last time.

"Shouldn't they answer? I mean, we're still up in the air. They have to be awake, right?"

"The plane's probably on autopilot," I say, a sinking feeling in my stomach. The pilots are out cold too.

"It's flying itself?" Rebecca asks.

I nod. "But it can't land on its own."

I can feel the old lady staring at me. I don't like it.

I want to go make sure my mom's okay—the need to check on her makes me want to jump out of my skin—but I can't. What if the old lady notices me heading to the crew bunk? I don't want my mom to be her next target.

"We need to figure out our next steps," Kiara says.

"That's easy: choose a sacrifice," the old woman says.

"My internet's not working." Yara pointedly ignores the old woman and holds up her phone.

"Same," Billy says.

Which means we have an unconscious flight crew, a locked cockpit door, and no way of communicating with the outside world. We really are on our own.

I glance at the ceiling. *Please, Mom, be okay up there. We need you.*

"Are we going to decide what to do now or what?" Rebecca folds her arms across her chest. "The clock is ticking." She points to the TV screens on the seatbacks.

2:53:39.

2:53:38.

2:53:37.

"Not with her listening to everything we say," Jack says.

The old lady chuckles.

Rebecca gestures at the rest of the cabin. "There's no place for us to talk where she won't hear."

Try the bathroom.

Emily's voice again.

Is it really her?

"We could put her in the bathroom," I say. "It locks from the outside. She can't do anything dangerous in there."

"Yeah," Yara agrees. "And we could play music outside the door. Between that and the plane noise, she won't hear anything." She peers at me from over the top of her phone and nods approvingly.

Rebecca puts her hands on her hips. "Okay. Spencer, you and Billy put the old lady in the back galley bathroom."

"Whoa, whoa, whoa. Who decided you're in charge?" Kiara squeezes past Andrew into the aisle.

"Here we go," Spencer murmurs to Billy.

Rebecca shrugs. "I'm class valedictorian and I just got early acceptance to Yale. I'm easily the smartest person on this plane. Why wouldn't I take charge?"

Kiara snorts. "Class valedictorian hasn't been announced yet."

Rebecca lets out a laugh. "Aww, do you really think you're still in the running? That's adorable, given that I scored higher than you on the advanced anatomy midterm."

"You don't know what you're talking about, so shut up," Kiara growls.

Rebecca examines her perfectly manicured nails. "Your student number is four-seven-seven-nine-five. Mr. Baldwin posts all his grades by student number and you got ninety-seven percent. I had a perfect score. So my GPA is higher. Besides, no way the school's going to allow someone who's on probation for stealing fundraising money to be the valedictorian."

"Cut it out, Rebecca." Andrew gets between her and Kiara—probably because Kiara looks like she's ready to knock Rebecca out.

This isn't good. People say things they shouldn't when they're stressed, things they might regret forever. I should know. I clear my throat to get everyone's attention.

"We need to figure out how to get through this flight without anyone else getting hurt. We can't do that if we're fighting," I say.

"Devon's right," Carter says.

"But someone has to be in charge, or it'll be chaos." Rebecca sniffs. "I'm the most qualified. Everyone knows it."

"Untrue. Kiara's still class president," Andrew says. "Technically, she's already in charge of us."

"*Of course* you choose her—you're her boyfriend." Rebecca's foot taps impatiently. "But who else will? Devon, maybe. Only because she's trying to be some kind of Emily clone. I mean, check out her clothes. Her sister wore that outfit all the time. It's weird."

It feels like I've just been punched.

"Don't listen to her," Carter says.

"We should take a vote. That's the only way to decide properly," Mai says slowly. "Democratically."

"Okay, I nominate myself," Rebecca says.

"And I nominate Kiara," Andrew says.

Rebecca groans.

"I nominate Devon," Carter says.

Kiara and Rebecca gape at him.

"What are you doing? I don't want to be in charge," I say. It's the truth. Thwarting authority has always been more my thing, not becoming it.

Carter shrugs. "Your mom's a pilot on this airline. You've traveled on planes more than any of us. You have the most knowledge of safety procedures and stuff, right? You're the logical choice."

Hearing Carter mention my mom nearly gives me a heart attack. The old lady doesn't need a reminder that she's on board. She's watching me closely. Her eyes narrow.

Yara clears her throat. "I second Carter's nomination."

"Guys. No. I do not want this," I say.

The old lady is still staring at me. I can feel her trying to pry open my brain again.

Mentally, I drum out one of my favorite grooves from "Billion Dollar Babies," this really old Alice Cooper song, to keep her out.

My head is all sound. The old lady sneers, then flicks her gaze to Rebecca.

Rebecca bites her lip and looks away.

"Third," Jack says. He turns to face me, and I shake the drumbeats from my head to focus on what he's saying. "The fact that you don't want to lead makes you a good choice. You're not interested in a power grab."

My heart stutters the way it always does with Jack, whether I want it to or not. Is he trying to play nice to get me to reconsider him as a suspect? Because it won't work.

"I can advise," I say.

"No. If it's either of these other two, they will do nothing but oppose each other on everything," Yara says. "I mean, if Emily were here . . ."

She lets the thought trail off.

"Sorry, I just mean—"

"She would accept the nomination. You're right, she would." I swallow hard. The whole thwarting authority bit is the old me. That girl did too many things worth regretting. If her instinct is to run from this, I should do the opposite. The new me—the Emily version—embraces responsibility.

"Fine. I'll be part of the vote." I give Carter a dirty look.

"You're strong enough to do it. You always have been," he says, unfazed.

I don't feel strong. I'm scared. I don't want to die on this plane. But then, if I can get to Mom and wake her up, she can be in charge. The thought soothes my nerves a little. I just have to wait for the right moment to go to her.

"Put it to a vote already." Jeanne groans as she and Mai step into the aisle. She glances at the TV screen closest to her.

2:45:21.

2:45:20.

2:45:19.

I hate that stupid clock already. Time is hemorrhaging away.

"All in favor of Devon?" Yara raises her hand and looks around.

A dozen hands go up, but there are twenty-four of us standing here.

"In favor of me?" Rebecca smiles so the dimples in her cheeks show. When a second goes by and she's the only one who's raised her hand, she kicks the row of seats in front of her. Wes startles, then raises his hand.

Jeanne's hand shoots up. Then two more hands. Jeanne nudges Mai and Mai sighs and raises her hand.

"And for Kiara?" Andrew asks. She gets the remaining six, including mine.

Rebecca purses her lips petulantly but doesn't challenge the vote. The old lady keeps stealing away half her attention. Maybe it's wrong, but I'm relieved the old woman's focus is on her and not me.

Beside me, Kiara goes very still.

Is she mad I won? She's always volunteering for leadership-type stuff. I don't want her to be angry at me. She was Emily's best friend, and so I need her to be mine too.

"I wanted it to be you," I whisper.

She shakes her head and sighs. "It doesn't even matter. All I want is to get on the ground safely."

Andrew kisses her forehead. She leans into him.

"Okay, so it's decided," Spencer says. "You're in charge. Now what?"

Every single kid stares at me expectantly, like they believe I know how to deal with a psychotic old woman and a plane full of unconscious passengers. Being in charge sucks already. I need Mom. Please God, let her be awake when I get to the crew bunk. In the meantime, I've got to act like I have a plan.

"We should get the crew buckled into empty seats. For their safety," I say slowly. This is what my mom would do. "Then we put the old woman into the bathroom. Give ourselves some privacy."

"That works." Spencer nods thoughtfully as he shifts the weight off his bad knee and leans against the seatback beside him.

I bend over Shazia and gently lift her shoulders. "I think we should put the crew in business class. Closer to the front. In case we manage to wake them up, we want people with flight experience closest to the cockpit."

Jack picks up Shazia's feet, and together we carry her up front. Carter and Andrew get Carlos, and Wes and Billy carry Olivia up last. There are three empty rows in business class with two seats in each. We give Carlos his own row so we can lay him across the seats.

"He's still bleeding." Kiara lifts his uniform shirt to examine his chest. "I'm going to get the medical bag and see what I can do to stop it." She volunteered at the local hospital for the past few years to get her volunteer hours for school and is the only one of us with even a smidgen of medical expertise, so it makes sense she feels like she should help Carlos.

I stare at his chest. The bleeding has slowed some, but there

73

is a pinkish foam around one of the wounds. That can't be good. At least he's out cold and can't feel it. He looks almost peaceful. Maybe the smoke put him into some kind of stasis? I hold on to this tiny piece of hope like a lifeline. Kiara doesn't have anywhere near enough expertise for this. And the only doctor on board is unconscious. If Carlos isn't stabilized, he's going to die up here.

I rub Emily's locket and let my gaze drift to the ceiling. I try to channel not just my sister, but my mother as well. What does the crew do when there are no doctors on board? I think back on the conversations I've had with my mom about her job. There have been a lot. Too many. I've tuned out most of them.

Stupid, stupid, I silently chastise myself as I mentally list what I remember about emergencies.

Flight crews are on planes to keep the passengers safe. That's why they get some medical emergency training during their orientation. They have protocols. Loads of rules and regulations. Do they memorize all of that?

I look around the cabin, but I'm not sure what I'm trying to find. It's not like those protocols are written on the walls or anything.

Wait.

Not on the walls.

But maybe in the flight crew's tablets.

I hurry to the business class beverage cart. One of those tablets is propped on the top. The crew usually uses it to take payments for alcohol and stuff, but it stores lots of other things. Like safety procedures. The passenger manifest. It makes sense that there might be medical instructions as well.

But when I grab it and turn on the screen, the tablet's locked. *Crap.*

No way I can crack the passcode unless I have at least a rough idea of what it might be.

I stare at the flight crew. Which one of them does it belong to?

It's on the business class beverage cart, so it might be Shazia's.

I check the back of her name tag hoping maybe she keeps her passcode there. No, of course not. But what about facial recognition? Could the tablet have it? I swipe the screen to make it come back on and hold it up to Shazia's face. Nothing.

"Jack, can you open her eyes for me so I can access this?" I don't like having to ask him, but he's the person closest to me since he helped me carry Shazia.

Jack grimaces as he gently pries Shazia's eyelids open.

I hold the tablet up to her face for a second time. This has to work.

The home screen appears.

"Yesss," I say, smiling.

"What?" Jack leans over me so he can get a better look at the screen. His arm bumps my back and my body goes on high alert. Every nerve ending in me is hyperaware of how near he is. I put some space between us.

I examine the tablet's document folders. Bingo. There's one marked *Medical.*

"I've got the bag." Kiara drops it on the ground beside Carlos.

"This has instructions for all sorts of emergencies." I hand Kiara the tablet.

"I can help you bandage him up," Jack offers.

Kiara tilts her head and stares at me. There's an unspoken question in her eyes. She was Emily's best friend, and she knows I accused Jack of being her killer.

"You need someone to read the instructions to you." I shrug. Better he helps Kiara and stays out of my way.

I head to the back of the plane.

The old lady's head appears over the seatback in front of her.

"You're channeling your twin so well, young Devon. When they look at you, it's her they're seeing more and more. Pretty soon you will be nothing but a memory and only Emily will remain."

She raises an eyebrow at me. "There are better ways to destroy yourself. Give your body to me and really show your classmates how sorry you are about what happened on Halloween."

Under her steady gaze, my thoughts feel muddled. What she's saying almost makes sense, it . . .

"Get out of my head!" I yell, scrunching my eyes shut so I can't see her anymore. I start up my mental drumming again, that same song by Alice Cooper with the strong intro. I make each beat loud, loud, loud.

My brain fog lifts.

When I open my eyes, the other kids look at me like I'm losing it.

Maybe I am.

The old lady nearly took control.

She starts humming. And I guess she managed to burrow into my brain a little after all, because the tune isn't the one she was humming earlier in the flight.

It's my song.

CHAPTER 10

"WE NEED TO GET THE OLD LADY INTO THE BATHROOM NOW," I tell the others. I can't keep giving her unlimited access to my head.

Spencer nods. "Open the door and I'll get her in."

The old lady's gaze swivels slowly in his direction. She stares at him so intently that it's as if an army of invisible spiders crawls over my back, making me shiver. Inside my pocket the needles start vibrating like they're an extension of her. I want them out now.

"Come on," Spencer orders, but he's watching her with wide eyes. He must be feeling those spiders too. She's burrowing into all our brains. The thought is horrifying.

The old woman scooches past the unconscious air marshal and into the aisle in front of Spencer.

I slip past them both, being careful not to let any part of me come into contact with any part of her. The first thing I do is stash the knitting needles inside one of the galley cabinets. Then I open the door to the second bathroom behind economy, closest to the galley.

"Come on, you." Spencer pokes her in the back. "Get inside."

"Dorothy. My name's Dorothy."

"That's your name or the name of the lady whose body you're in?" I ask.

"Potato, po-tah-to." The old lady grins so her rotten tooth shows. "Same thing."

"Go on, get in there," Spencer orders. This time he pushes her roughly.

The old woman stumbles into the tiny bathroom, then turns around and sits regally on top of the closed toilet seat. "Have your fun while you can. Then I'll have mine." Her gaze flicks from Spencer to me. Her eyes glint with what I can only describe as pure malice. I slide the lock into place and then check it twice to make sure it's secure.

"She is creeptastic," Spencer mutters. "And nuttier than a squirrel turd."

I grab my backpack from my seat and pull out my phone and my travel-sized Bluetooth speaker. Then I flip through my play-lists until I find the one I want. It's a compilation of my favorite drum solos. I connect the speaker to my phone and crank the volume, then aim it at the tiny crack at the bottom of the door. It's not exactly soundproofing, but hopefully she won't be able to hear us talking if we're far enough away.

"Everyone." I raise my voice so I can be heard by the entire cabin. "Let's meet up in business class. Also, we need two volunteers to guard the bathroom door."

"I've got it," Spencer says.

Billy steps forward to volunteer too, but then Jeanne grabs his arm and leans her head against his bicep.

"No. I don't want you anywhere near her," she says. "And besides, I need you." She's practically whining.

Billy kisses the top of her head so briefly that his lips barely make contact with her hair. "Mai'll be up there with you. You won't be alone. And besides, you'll be able to see me the whole time."

"Or Mai can hang with me so you can go with her," Spencer offers.

Jeanne gives Mai a pleading look. "I need Billy with me. You go."

Mai looks thoroughly unamused.

"Or I can do it." Rebecca strides down the aisle.

"You want to volunteer?" I ask. "Why?"

"Because I need to make myself useful or my nerves will get the best of me," she says. There's a slight tremor in her lips. She breaks eye contact and stares at the row we just took the old lady from, at the air marshal sleeping there. I'm betting she's wishing we could somehow wake him up, because I'm wishing that too. I've never wanted an adult in charge so badly. This flight is getting more surreal by the moment. If the old lady can actually crash the plane and not just make us hallucinate that she can, things are going to get much worse in the next few hours. I'm not convinced any of us will be able to handle it.

"There's two of us and the door is locked. We'll be fine," Spencer says. "And if she tries to get out, I'll bash her in the head with this." He pulls a fire extinguisher off the galley wall. It's smaller than a normal extinguisher, which makes it more easily manageable to wield as a weapon, especially for someone as big as Spencer.

"Okay." I step around the crimson stains on the galley floor where Carlos had been laid out. "If you pick up the phone on the wall, you can listen in. Just make sure the volume is quiet enough that she can't hear."

"Hey, Devon?" Spencer calls out.

I turn around. "Yeah?"

"For someone who didn't want to be in charge, you're already doing a kickass job."

Rebecca makes a face behind him.

"Thanks." I want to believe him, but there's this knot in my gut that won't go away. The old lady's been too cooperative.

What is she really up to?

I'm afraid to find out.

The front galley of our plane is bigger than most. The roominess is one of the things Sky Royal brags about. Still, it's tight, with twenty-two out of the twenty-four of us trying to huddle into it. Eight of us manage to fit in the actual galley, but the remaining kids spill out into the aisle and the narrow space behind the wall at the front of business class.

I glance at the galley cabinets and the door to the crew bunk. I can't get my mom out of my mind. She hasn't come out on her own. Chances are good that she's unconscious like all the other adults, but I'm still hoping somehow she isn't, that she's just slept through all the drama. As soon as this meeting is over, I'm going up there to find out.

Kiara's still with Carlos. She's bandaged his chest, but the blood is already seeping through. She shoots me a look. His skin is so ashen my stomach flips. He is going to need way more medical intervention than a couple of bandages and some antiseptic.

Jack's a few feet away, holding Shazia's tablet, his forehead puckered in concentration as he scrolls through whatever medical emergency document he's looking at. I doubt there are any instructions for what to do when a psychotic granny uses knitting needles like meat tenderizers on a person, but it's all we've got.

Just beyond the galley, Andrew is slumped in one of the business class seats. A sheen of sweat glistens on his forehead and upper lip, and he's gripping an airsickness bag like his life depends on it. His journal bounces up and down on his lap as his leg taps furiously. He's finally unraveling.

I look past him to where Yara is recording. As if sensing me watching her, she looks over the top of her phone at me with shell-shocked eyes. We're all just trying to process what's happening, aren't we? Recording is her way, I guess.

Jeanne and Mai close the curtains between first class and the economy section of the cabin so most of the unconscious passengers are out of sight. Jeanne glances back at the handful of seats that are still occupied.

"Am I the only one creeped out by them?" She rubs her arms like she's freezing and needs the friction to get warm. "They look dead."

"They do," Billy admits, "but I'm not moving anyone else. We have more important stuff to deal with right now."

Since I'm apparently in charge, I stand at the center of the galley and prepare to talk about the loose set of plans I've managed to cobble together in the past few minutes. It's weird up here—almost like a stage. Only none of the people in front of me wants to be here watching me or going through this. All these kids I've known since elementary school look like they've aged ten years. It makes them seem like strangers. I lift the phone from the galley wall and make sure Spencer and Rebecca are listening in, then pass it to Carter to hold.

What am I supposed to say to comfort them? What would Emily say? I rub my sister's locket between my fingers and try to channel her. Emily was always taking care of everyone. Making dinners on the nights Mom or Dad was running late. Babysitting the Miller kids next door. Volunteering at Andrew's charity restaurant with Kiara. She would try to take care of everyone on board this plane. She would keep them safe, help them feel less scared.

I'm almost dizzy with nerves. It's strange—when I'm on a stage behind my drum set, I am completely at ease, even if there are hundreds of people in the audience, but standing here, I feel vulnerable and exposed.

"What are we supposed to do?" Wes asks when I don't start talking, his voice going up an octave on the last two words. "I mean, what's the plan here?"

I take a deep breath. *Here goes.*

"So, I've been thinking. What happened earlier—when we thought the plane was crashing? Was it really supernatural? Or some sort of mass hallucination? Because some stuff just doesn't add up," I say.

I'm talking through my thoughts in real time, no self-editing. At first I was convinced the old lady was telling the truth about who and what she is, but the more I pick apart what's happened, the more doubts I have.

"What do you mean?" Yara aims her phone at me.

"Can you stop recording right now?" Jeanne asks, her voice quavering. "Please?"

"I don't think I should." Yara pushes the sleeves of her hoodie up her arms and re-aims the camera at Jeanne. "It's important to document everything. For when they investigate this flight on the ground."

Jeanne lets out a sob. "Because you think we're gonna die? This isn't one of your horror mockumentaries, some B-rate *Blair Witch* on a plane, Yara. This is real life. And I don't want to die."

"Hey, hey. Let's not get hysterical. No one's going to die," I say, but even I'm not convinced. Panic is a bass drum banging away inside my chest. I keep mentally replaying the plane dropping, everyone being ripped out into the sky. For a hallucination, it was heart-stoppingly real. I need to believe that's all it was, though. Otherwise, what chance do we really have here?

Jeanne glares at me, teary-eyed. "Yeah? How do you know? You heard the old lady. We need to choose someone for her to possess or she'll crash the plane. So that's what we need to do." She's practically convulsing, she's shaking so hard.

Billy puts his arms around her, and she buries her head in his chest. When her sobs get more intense, deep furrows appear between his eyebrows as he looks over the top of her hair at Mai. She mirrors his concern. Jeanne is halfway to hysterical. This same girl seemed totally unflappable before today, the sort of person who goes through her days with a permanent bounce in her step, who's the life of just about every party.

I can't stop to give her time to calm down, though. Every minute we don't agree on a plan increases the chances of us not surviving this flight.

"But how do we know she can do it?" I ask. "I mean, think about it. The shared vision we had of the plane falling? What if it was some sort of group hypnosis or something? I mean, she did all that humming. And clacking those knitting needles of hers together at the start of the flight. They could've been some sort of trigger to put us under. Because the plane didn't actually fall, did it? So then it's not irrational to think she's trying to manipulate us into believing she's some kind of magical, supernatural creature. If she really was that powerful, how come she couldn't escape those plasti-cuffs? I mean, there's a ton of YouTube videos about how to escape from those things *without* supernatural abilities, and she's still cuffed."

Jack looks up from Shazia's tablet. "But what about the smoke that came out of her mouth? Or the fact that she knew something bad about Carlos—like she could read his mind."

"We saw *some* smoke come out of her mouth," I say. "But is anyone one hundred percent sure all of it came from her? This could be part of some kind of terrorist attack. A coordinated detonation of gas canisters timed to make it *seem* like all the smoke came from her." I straighten my shoulders. The longer I keep to this train of thought, the more it makes sense and the calmer I feel.

"And as for Carlos—I don't know," I admit. "But so-called psychics can read people really well. There are all these documentaries about it, debunking their abilities. So maybe she's like them?"

"But why did only the adults and little kids get knocked out?" Carter asks. "And what's her endgame? I mean, if she can't really possess someone, why go to all the trouble to get us to believe she can? If it's a terrorist attack, why not give us her actual demands— I mean, real-world ones?"

I shrug. "I don't have all the answers. But don't you think it's worth investigating before we seriously consider sacrificing one of us? Because if she's just a person, then there's no possession. Then this is something else. Something real-world awful, and if that's the case, I guarantee none of us are making it out of this cabin alive unless we can keep her contained and break whatever hold she has on us. It's the only way we can safely land this plane."

"I agree." Andrew raises his airsickness bag like we're taking another vote. "We have a little bit of time. Exhausting every other possibility before we give in to her demand is just logical. In fact, it's the only thing that makes any sense so far." His pale face contorts, and he hunches out of sight. A second later, he vomits so loudly everyone can hear.

"Oh no, Drew." Kiara leaves Carlos's side to tend to him.

Yara leans over the seat to record the vomit. "Very visceral," she murmurs.

"Do you mind?" Kiara snaps at her.

"Not at all." Instead of moving away, Yara holds the phone down closer to Andrew.

"Stop!" Kiara bats the phone out of Yara's hand. It clatters to the floor.

"If you broke the screen or the camera's screwed up in any way," Yara says, "I'm gonna—"

Before she can finish the sentence, someone screams.

CHAPTER 11

"SHE'S IN MY HEAD! GET HER OUT OF MY HEAD!" REBECCA IS ON her knees in the back galley, holding her head with her hands, rocking. There is blood running down her chin, onto the front of her shirt.

The bathroom door is still locked.

The old woman is still contained.

My drum playlist is still playing on my phone. It's exactly where I left it.

But there is one thing missing.

"Where's Spencer?" I crouch beside Rebecca. She nods at the second bathroom and the *Occupied* indicator above the lock before she fists her hands and hits the sides of her head.

"Get out, get out, GET OUT!" she shouts. A mix of blood and saliva sprays out of her mouth.

"Rebecca. Can you hear us?" Jack leans over me and snaps his fingers in front of her face.

"Rebecca?" I squeeze her hands.

She blinks. Tears stream down her cheeks and mix with the blood on her chin. "Sh-sh-she was inside my head. Making me think such awful things." She scans the crowd of kids who rushed to the back of the plane with me when we heard the scream. "She said the longer we take to choose someone, the more we'll suffer. She sh-sh-showed me."

Her hands slip out from under mine. She presses them over her mouth.

"Suffer how?" Kiara asks.

Rebecca's head swivels side to side again as she silently mouths "No, no, no," blood still pouring from her lips.

"What did she show you? Rebecca?" I shake her gently to try to jar her out of her panic. Then over my shoulder to any-one close enough to listen: "I need a towel. And can someone please shut off my phone?" The clamorous music is putting me on edge.

"Here." Carter hands me a towel from the beverage cart. Very gently I dab at the blood on Rebecca's face and mouth.

She shudders. "She made me think my teeth were rotting. I thought if they stayed inside my mouth, they would poison me. . . . It was *so real.* I mean, I couldn't control myself." She stares helplessly at me. "I found this little hammer in the galley and I just . . ." She mimes hitting her mouth with it.

I stare at the plastic hammer on the floor beside her. The crew uses it to break up the ice for beverage service. My mouth goes dry as I imagine her bashing away at her teeth.

Rebecca moans and starts rocking again. "It hurt so bad. Part of me was screaming to stop, but I couldn't stop. I couldn't . . ." She runs her fingers over her front teeth. One of the pointy eye-teeth is missing. When she realizes it's gone, she starts screaming all over again.

"Oh, God." Kiara closes her eyes and looks away.

Everyone falls silent.

That's when we hear her. The old woman. She's humming my Alice Cooper song again.

"Shut up!" Billy hits the bathroom door with his fist.

She doesn't listen.

Billy reaches for the lock.

"Don't!" I yell. "What if she managed to get out of her cuffs?"

Billy's hand hesitates above the lock for a moment before he exhales heavily and lets it drop to his side again.

"Uh, people? Why isn't Spencer coming out of the other bathroom?" Yara asks softly, eyeing the second bathroom door. "With her screaming like she was, you'd think he would've run out of there to see what was going on."

We all stare at the second bathroom door. Did the old lady do something to him too?

Billy walks over to the door.

"Dude. Is that a good idea?" Jack murmurs.

"He had a fire extinguisher before," I whisper. "To use on the old lady in case she escaped. And it's not out here, which means he's got it in there with him."

What if she's making him hallucinate too? Tricking him into attacking us the second we open that door?

Billy swallows hard, then raps gently on the door.

"Spence?"

The silence is deafening.

I listen so hard for even the slightest noise that my ears throb.

Billy tries again, knocking a little harder this time.

"Spence? You in there?"

Jack nudges his back. "Of course he's in there. Where else could he be?" Then he pushes past Billy and pounds on the door.

"Spence. Open up."

More silence.

"So now what?" Billy locks eyes with Jack.

Jack glances around the galley, then stoops and picks up the ice hammer. It looks almost harmless, less a weapon than a kids' toy.

"Why do you need that?" Billy stares at the hammer. "It's Spencer."

"If she got into his head, he might hurt us, right?" Jack glances over his shoulder at us. "Everybody get back. Just in case."

Suddenly, there's the sound of the toilet flushing.

The door flies open.

Kiara and Mai gasp.

Spencer steps out toting the fire extinguisher, a glassy look in his eyes. He's wearing his earbuds. Whatever music he's listening to is so loud I can hear it from where I'm standing.

Spencer's eyes widen when he sees us. He pops his earbuds out and tucks them into his pocket. "What?"

"You were supposed to be out here guarding the bathroom door," I say, heat rushing into my cheeks. "With Rebecca."

He frowns. "I was. But then I needed a second."

"For what?" I demand.

He snorts. "Do I really have to spell it out for you?" But when he sees everyones' faces, the smirk vanishes. "What?"

Mai pulls Rebecca forward and Spencer whistles softly. "What happened to you?"

Rebecca glares at him.

"Tell me." Spencer limps over to her so he can get a better look at her damaged mouth, and his jaw clenches. "Damn."

"She said the old lady got inside her head," I tell him. "Maybe if you had been out here, you could've stopped her before she knocked one of her teeth out." Anger courses through me, white-hot and as familiar as an old friend. Before I can stop myself, I'm letting it spill out of my mouth and poison my words. "This is your fault. If you hadn't been so careless, so utterly stupid, she'd be okay. But that's too much to expect, isn't it? Because stupid is your default setting."

Spencer flinches. The deep hurt in his eyes makes my gut twist. I went too far.

He didn't force Rebecca to break her tooth, the old woman did. The truth is, I'm terrified. If the old woman's powers of hypnosis can not only give us hallucinations but manipulate our thoughts to make us hurt ourselves, does it really matter how she's managing it? I mean, what chance do we have of surviving?

Everyone's looking to me to figure out what we're supposed to do. My throat and chest tighten, and my pulse races. I'm not this person, their leader. Emily could've been, but not me. No matter how hard I keep trying to be like her, this situation has my self-control fissuring. The old me, the one with a venom tongue, who speaks before she thinks, is seeping through the cracks.

"I'm sorry," Spencer says. "I thought she was secure. I didn't know." He eyes the old lady's bathroom door for a second, then hits it with a fist. The door shudders.

Inside, the old lady is still humming, just loud enough to be heard. Her voice has gravel laced through it, a ribbon of darkness that sends a chill snaking up my spine. I want to run so badly. Hide in the crew bunk room with my mom and let the others figure out what to do. I take a step backward, then one more. The others are too focused on the door, on the creepy humming. I could slip away. No one would know. God, I'm such a hypocrite. I just yelled at Spencer for leaving Rebecca alone and here I am wanting to abandon everyone.

Stay. Emily's voice reverberates through my brain so loudly I clap a hand to my mouth to keep from crying out.

"What is it?"

Yara is beside me, her phone camera trained on me, a look of alarm on her face.

"Don't record me." I block the lens with my hands.

She bites her lip and looks back at her phone. "I wasn't this time, I swear." She slips the phone into her pocket. "What happened just then? You looked . . . strange."

I listen for Emily's voice again, but it's gone. I know because my head is emptier somehow. It felt like Emily was right beside me. I don't even believe in ghosts—I never have—but right now I want to believe. Because if she is here, there are things I need to say to her.

If she is here, I owe it to her to stay. I owe her so much more than that, but it's a start. It's enough for now.

CHAPTER 12

"EVERYONE UP FRONT," I SAY, MAKING MY VOICE SOUND MORE confident than I feel. "No one stays back here this time. No one goes anywhere near that bathroom door alone."

"Just leave her unguarded?" Andrew asks. "What if she manages to get out?"

"We can leave the curtain in business class open. The plane isn't so big that we won't see or hear her."

I reach out and touch Spencer's arm. "I'm sorry for what I said. I sort of lost it for a second."

Spencer's jaw flexes and for a moment I think he's going to tell me off, but then he shrugs. "It's okay. I screwed up. I deserved it."

"No, you didn't."

He holds up his hand. "Stop, okay? We're good. Go up front. I'm right behind you." Judging from the tension lingering in his jaw, we're not one hundred percent good, but I don't know what else to do to make it better right now.

"Okay, so we have to break her mental connection with us," I say once we're all huddled into the front galley and business class again.

"Still think she's hypnotizing us somehow?" Kiara gently guides Rebecca to the business class bathroom. "Can someone hand me some gauze? It's in the medical emergency bag."

Jack stoops to rifle through the bag, then throws Kiara a few packs of sterile gauze.

"And a bottle of water," Kiara calls.

Carter goes to the beverage cart, grabs a water, and hands it to her. Then he goes back to the cart and pulls out a drawer. "Dude." Carter whistles. "Check it out." There are rows and rows of travel-sized alcohol bottles inside. "Anyone else need a drink? Because I need a drink." He grabs a whiskey, twists it open, and downs the contents in one go. Wincing, he raises another bottle to the rest of us like an offering.

"Yeah, pass me one," Spencer says eagerly.

"We're not supposed to drink those." Wes glances nervously back toward the seat where our chaperones, Mrs. Sicmaszko and Mr. Lewton, are passed out cold. "I mean, none of us are twenty-one."

Spencer snorts humorlessly. "Dude, who the hell is gonna stop us?"

Wes glares at Spencer.

Billy grabs one for himself and then passes one to Jeanne, then Mai.

"Yeah, but given the circumstances, is it a good idea?" Yara asks. "I mean, if people start getting drunk—"

"From these?" Billy snorts. "They're miniature. No one's getting drunk off these."

Spencer raises his bottle and tips it at his best friend. "Challenge accepted."

"Devon, heads up." Carter tosses me a bottle. I catch it. It's a tiny vodka. I look over at Jack. That's what we were drinking at the Halloween party, the night we hooked up at Jeanne's house—or, at least, it's what *he* was drinking. I could barely manage more than one shot before my eyes started getting all jiggly and my head felt like it was floating. It was the closest I've ever been to getting drunk, which is to say, I've never gotten very close at all. I'm not much of a drinker. This always surprises people. They assume because I'm in a band, I'm a massive partyer. But the thing is, I was too busy trying to play a perfect set, to get discovered and become famous. It was more important than partying, than school, than family. It was everything. Until the night Emily died.

I tuck the vodka inside my pocket. I need to think clearly right now. When I look up, Jack is watching me. He gives me a tentative smile. Is he remembering that night too? I frown and look away.

Billy helps Carter pass out the rest of the bottles. Most kids only take one, except for Andrew who takes two. He's still all pasty and clammy-looking from his vomit session. He downs both bottles quick and then slumps into a seat and closes his eyes.

I grab a bag of pretzels and hand them to him. "These might help settle your stomach."

He manages a weak smile. "Thanks." There are tears in his eyes.

I pat his shoulder. "Hey, we'll figure out how to get through this."

"What if we don't? What if we die?" He wipes away a tear. "I'm not ready. I mean, what happens to us after? What if I haven't been good enough to go to heaven?"

"If anyone's been good enough, it's you," I tell him, smiling. "You created a restaurant to feed homeless people. That has to get you in."

I can tell he doesn't believe me. What I don't get is why he's so hard on himself.

"Do you believe in hell?" Andrew asks abruptly, his voice tight.

The question blindsides me. It isn't that I haven't thought about it. I've thought about it a lot, especially after Emily. Does Andrew know what happened between me and my sister on Halloween?

"Yes," I say slowly. "But not in the fiery-pit place. I believe you can be in hell right here. On earth." I swallow hard and try to blink away the tears suddenly gathering in my eyes. This is the truest statement I've made since my sister died. Hell is where I've been all these months. "I don't know about the rest—about whether God exists or not. Sometimes I catch myself praying to him anyway. Like that makes any sense, right? Praying to a being that keeps allowing bad things to happen, who doesn't seem to answer those prayers no matter how badly you want him to. I mean, he isn't intervening right now, is he? But then, if the creature inside that old lady can exist, I guess it's logical that there is some version of God in existence too. I'm just not sure if it's the God I've been taught about. And yeah, I guess places like heaven or hell can exist too."

Andrew's tears fall faster. "Sometimes I have these nightmares about ending up in hell." He rakes a hand through his hair and stares at the floor rather than at me. "After I've had a fight with my parents or been mean to my brother. Done something terribly wrong. And the nightmares are so real." His hands grip his journal so tightly his fingernails dig into the leather and leave marks. "I don't want to die tonight, Devon."

He sinks his head into his hands. There is something so raw and vulnerable about the way he's sitting there. I've never seen Andrew like this. We've barely talked—definitely not about anything as deep as this.

It's like he's putting all the guilt and worry I've felt all these months into words. I can't stop shaking. The moment is too much.

"Devon. Can I talk to you for a second in private?" Jack taps me on the shoulder. "I think I have an idea."

I look from him to Andrew.

Jack frowns.

"Hey, are you okay?"

I wrap my arms around my chest to keep from trembling.

"I'm fine," I lie. "But maybe I should stay with Andrew for a few more minutes?"

Andrew waves me away. "I'll be fine. Seriously. Go."

As if to prove it, he gets up and strides to the back of the plane. He tosses his journal into his seat then heads in Kiara's direction. He would probably rather discuss all this with her. I'd be lying if I said I wasn't relieved to see him go. I'm not good with other people's emotions—especially when they so closely mirror my own.

"I was looking through the flight attendant's tablet," Jack says when we're far enough away that no one can hear. His face is close to mine and the scent of whatever soap he uses lingers in the air between us. It is immediately comforting—but it shouldn't be. I take a step back to make some space.

"It's got everything, including the flight manifest," Jack says. "The old lady said her name was Dorothy, right? She was sitting in fifteen B." He tilts the tablet so I can see.

"Dorothy Burdon."

"If you click here, her ticket information comes up. Her address. Phone number."

She lives on Carraway Court in Souderton, Pennsylvania.

Somehow, seeing her address and phone number steals away some of my fear. It's so normal. It makes me think I'm right about her mass-hypnotizing us. The creature bit has got to be a lie. Something to freak us out and distract us from the truth, make us think there's no way we can resist her. I mean, would a supernatural creature really live in the suburbs? It seems absurd.

"There's something else." Jack closes the passenger manifest and opens another document, one from the emergency files. "The medical bag has all these drugs in it. And these files have pretty detailed descriptions of what each of them is for. Instructions for how to administer them. The proper dosage, I mean. I was trying to figure out what we should give Carlos—and now Rebecca, maybe—for pain. In case they need it."

I stare at the tablet.

"Okay."

His eyes flit from the tablet to mine. "And then I got to thinking about the old woman. Maybe we could . . ."

"Drug her?"

He nods. "She can't hypnotize anyone if she's out cold."

It's a solid idea. But it's risky. I don't like that Jack's the one who thought of it.

Jack clears his throat. "Listen. I know you don't trust me. You want to figure out what happened to Emily and I'm the most logical choice of suspects."

This is an understatement. It isn't just that he was at the party. It's that his car had damage to the front hood that wasn't there before Halloween. He was drinking that night. And then he disappeared for months. Decided to homeschool. Every single thing he's done points to his guilt. I still don't get why the police cleared him. They've never given my parents and me the details. And Jack hasn't exactly come clean either about what happened to his car and where he's been.

He glances around at everyone else to see if they're listening. No one is. They're too busy drinking.

"The night we were together, I was pretty trashed. You remember, right?" Jack shakes his head. "I was messed up at most of the parties I went to. I know I had a bad reputation around school."

I hate myself for it, but that reputation is part of what intrigued me in the first place—he was wild in a way I can't seem to allow myself to be.

He runs a hand through his hair and swallows hard. "I drove myself home from the party. It was the dumbest thing I've ever done. But I didn't hit your sister." He clenches his jaw. "I made it all the way home and ran into my own garage door. My parents found me passed out in the front seat."

His eyes lock on mine. "I remember leaving the party. I never saw Emily on the road. She was still at Jeanne's house with you."

I shake my head. "You were drunk. You can't know that for sure."

"Don't you think that if there was even the slightest chance that it might be me, the cops wouldn't have taken me off their list of suspects?"

"How am I supposed to believe this?" I nearly shout. "You never came to talk to me or my parents to clear it up. Why? If you're so innocent, why couldn't you do that?"

He presses his lips together and looks down.

I throw my hands in the air.

"You know what? Whether or not I believe you doesn't matter right now. What matters is making sure no one dies tonight. Do you think any of these drugs are the kind that can knock the old lady out?"

Jack shrugs miserably. "I haven't found one so far."

"That's because you're looking in the wrong place," Spencer says, glancing at both of us with one eyebrow raised. "You two good?"

"Peachy," I snap. "What're you talking about, Spencer?"

He drops a pill bottle into Jack's hand. "It's Valium. Found it in one of the passenger's bags. There's always at least one person on a flight who's freaked out about flying and brings these. Grind up the pills and mix them with a little water and we can inject them into the old bat's veins. She'll be out in no time. But you gotta be precise about the dose. Too much and we don't just knock her out. We kill her."

"How do you know all this?" I ask.

"I watch a lot of episodes of *Intervention*—you know, the show that follows addicts around and shows their families confronting them about their drug use." He shrugs. "They go into a lot of detail."

I clap my hands together to get everyone's attention.

"We have a way to stop the old woman. Jack, tell them."

Jack's cheeks are bright red—have been since our talk. He repeats what he told me. Then Spencer goes over his recipe for sedating the old lady.

"It won't work." Rebecca steps out of the bathroom. Her eyes are red from crying and her mouth is stuffed with gauze, so her words come out a little jumbled. "There's no way to stop her except to give her what she wants. It's the only way she'll leave us alone."

"You can't know that for sure," Kiara says. "She messed with your head back there and scared you into thinking that."

Rebecca shakes her head emphatically. "It wasn't hypnosis. I could feel her clawing at my brain, a piece of her worming her way in." She shivers. "I felt it, that creature—the thing inside of her. It's not human. And we cannot defeat it." Her voice is flat, void of emotion, but it's her eyes that worry me most, the complete and utter resignation in them.

"I know you believe that," I tell her, "but if there's even the slightest chance that you're wrong, we have to try."

CHAPTER 13

I LIFT SHAZIA'S ID CARD UP TO THE LOCK ON THE CABINET THAT leads to the crew's bunk room. There's an audible click as the lock disengages and I open the door. The ladder inside is steeped in darkness.

"Mom?" I call out in a whisper, then steel my nerves and make my voice louder. "Mom?"

Please wake up. Please answer. I need you.

The silence above me remains thick, oppressive.

I look back toward the main cabin, then step into the cabinet and close the door behind me. I can still hear some of what's going on, but it's muffled. Kiara's voice is clearest. I left her in charge while I'm in here, and it's obvious she's taking full advantage, handing out orders.

The truth is, she's more capable at leading than I am. With Spencer's help, Jack is prepping the sedative, figuring out the proper dosage of Valium; we don't want to give the old lady too much if knocking her out could mean hurting the unconscious passengers, or worse. Carter and Mai are on overhead-bin duty to see if they can find any luggage belonging to Dorothy, some clue that could help us figure out why she's doing this. Jeanne and Billy are looking for possible weapons on board in case we need them. And Yara and Wes are trying to keep everyone else calm by handing out snacks and drinks. With twenty-four of us, we can get more done if some people just sit down and stay out of the way. This means most of the other kids are seated—along with Andrew. He's still sick and barely able to do more than rest in place with his eyes closed.

We've decided to drug the old woman near the end of the second hour of the flight, which is in about thirty minutes. That should be just enough time for us to prepare the medicine and figure out the safest way to give it to her. I have until then to check on my mom.

I hang Shazia's lanyard around my neck and start climbing the ladder. It's a short trip. The bunk room is less than seven feet up from the main cabin. I take out my phone and click on the flashlight, then shine it into the pitch-black space. It's smaller and narrower than I expected. When Mom first told me there were secret rooms on some planes for the crew to take breaks in, I pictured a big open space, like a regular bedroom. But this is more like something you might find on a submarine—basically a narrow hallway with bunks set into either wall, cubbies at the far end for personal items, and a fire extinguisher beside it. On the wall by the ladder is an enormous flashlight. I make a mental note to remember this stuff is up here, in case we need backups for the emergency equipment in the main cabin.

I suck in a breath when I see Mom and race over to her.

She's in the first bunk, lying on her back with her arms folded across her stomach. Given the narrowness of the space and the closeness of the wall and ceiling, it's almost like she's in a coffin.

"Mom?" Very gently, I shake her shoulder. "Mom." I shake harder. Then even harder. "Wake up."

No response.

She's so still. My heart twists painfully. What if she's not unconscious? What if she's dead? It feels like I'm the one free-falling now, not the plane. Like I'm losing my grip.

I grab hold of my mom's wrist and press my fingers to it. She has a pulse. I sag back onto my knees and exhale. She's just like all the rest of the adults.

It's enough to make my head swim. I'm so relieved she's alive and yet so utterly disappointed at the same time. As long as there was even a slim possibility that she was only sleeping, we weren't completely on our own. I could manage being in charge. I convinced myself that if I got overwhelmed, I could come to get her and let her take over. It was stupid and naive. I get that now.

I push a wayward strand of hair out of her face. Even knocked out, she looks troubled. There's a permanent furrow between her eyebrows and deep lines around her mouth. Her lips have been pulled downward into a frown ever since Emily died. She seems so much older, worn, and a little fragile.

Her phone is beside her on the bunk, and she has her earbuds in—well, she still has one of them in. The other is caught in her hair. I pick it up and put it into my ear, then hold the phone up to her face so it'll turn on. I check to see what she was listening to.

My throat tightens the second Emily's face appears. Mom was watching a video. I rewind it and press Play. It's of Emily and me when we were little. We're in the woods across the street from our house, running over the snowy ground. We look silly clad in our snow boots and Disney princess nightgowns under our coats. Dad's leading the way, so Mom must've been the one filming.

I see Emily glance back at the camera. She's around eight, maybe.

"Happy Christmas!" she shouts at the camera, her cheeks ruddy from running, her eyes so bright they sparkle.

Emily always said "Happy Christmas," not *merry*. She insisted it sounded better. I think it's just because it suited her more, the word *happy*. She was almost always smiling, at least when she was little. Less often the past few years. It was like she was keeping more of herself private from me by then.

"Devon, say 'Happy Christmas,'" Mom calls, and the joy in her voice is unmistakable. Mom has always lived for the holidays—until this past year.

The me on camera turns and sticks her tongue out, then laughs like a banshee as she races past Emily to catch up to Dad, her wild curls rippling out behind her, the edge of her nightgown rimmed with dirt from where it hits the heels of her boots.

Emily looks into the camera and rolls her eyes, but she's smiling still.

I know what the video is about now. A lump forms in my throat.

Our tree house appears up ahead.

Video Emily and I squeal with delight.

The next bit is taken from the top of the ladder, near the floor of the tree house. Mom's laughing softly from behind the camera. Emily and I are holding hands and dancing in a circle while Dad is sitting cross-legged in the corner, looking pleased with himself.

That was our best Christmas. That tree house became our sisters-only clubhouse, the place where we shared secrets and played pretend, where I always felt closest to Emily.

I wipe the tears from my eyes. Mom's watching this clip because it was from before Emily and I started drifting apart. Three years later, Emily and I started middle school. Things changed. She was popular and into getting good grades, participating in sports and clubs, and I was . . . different. I got obsessed with the drums and music. I hated sports and despised school.

Her default was to please people. Mine was to antagonize them.

She rarely got into trouble. I never seemed to get out of it.

It's no surprise people liked to be around her more—not just people, but my parents. I get why. And it wasn't like she was *trying* to be the favorite on purpose. But still, I couldn't stop resenting her.

I replay the video one more time, then shut off Mom's phone. I turn so I'm sitting with my back to Mom's bunk. It's easier to talk to her when I don't have to face her. I lean my head against her arm and stare up at the ceiling.

"I wish I could redo it all. That I had been less selfish. I wish I could take Halloween night back, but also so many other times too." I continue to stare at the ceiling and try to keep the tears building inside my eyes from falling. "She should've lived. I should've watched over her the way she did me. Then you and Dad wouldn't be in so much pain."

I hug my knees to my chest. "And now I might not get the chance to make up for what I did. We could die tonight. I'm trying to keep it from happening, but I don't really know what I'm doing. I'm not sure the plan we've come up with is going to work. And if it doesn't, how do we do what the old lady is asking? Can we really choose one of us to sacrifice? But then how can we not? I can't let Dad lose us too. He'd be all alone."

I rest my chin on my knees. "I don't know what to do. Help me figure out what to do."

I don't even know who I'm talking to anymore: Mom, God, Emily, myself.

I stare into the darkness.

"Please show me."

Of course, no one answers.

My fingers and toes feel numb. It's so much colder up here than down in the cabin.

Shivering, I turn and crawl in next to my mom and pull her blanket up around us both. It's been months since I've been this close to her. I lean my head against her chest so I can hear her heartbeat.

"I'm going to try to save us," I say.

Suddenly, her phone lights up. A text notification appears.

But that's impossible. The internet's down.

It's from Emily's phone. How? Her phone is on her dresser in her bedroom. It's not like Dad would ever dream of contacting

Mom with it, not when he knows exactly how much that would upset her. I suck in a breath and open the text.

Needles.

One word.

As I stare at the screen, the little dots show up to indicate someone's typing. Then the whole screen fills up with that same word. Needles. Over and over and over, more than a hundred times.

The hairs on the back of my neck stand on end as the bunk room fills with a familiar smell. Emily's perfume. The only one she ever wore because she always liked the idea of having a signature scent—vanilla and sandalwood with an almost smoky note.

"Emily?"

My voice seems to get swallowed up, like the bunk room is covered in soundproofing. Even the air is different. Thicker, somehow.

Is she really here?

I wait for an answer, but nothing happens.

I look at the text again and type a response.

Emily?

Again, nothing.

I try one more time.

I don't understand. Explain.

I wait.

No answer.

And then the air warms and the weird, insulated quality of the space dissipates until there is only the subtle, lingering scent of my sister's perfume.

I inhale and close my eyes.

"Is it really you?" I whisper.

I'm not even expecting an answer, if I'm honest. I think I'm asking myself whether or not I believe it was her more than I'm looking for her to confirm it. It isn't my brain but my gut that answers yes.

But if she's here, why tonight?

Unless—wherever she is—she knows our lives are in danger. Then it makes sense why it feels like she's so present and why she's trying to make contact. Emily was the older twin by a only a few minutes, but even so, she was forever protecting me even when I didn't want her to.

I slip my mom's phone into my pocket and head for the ladder. Emily has to be talking about the old lady's knitting needles. I don't know why she wants me to have them or what I'm supposed to do with them once I do, but I know that she's somehow trying to keep me safe. This time, I'm going to listen to her.

CHAPTER 14

I SLIP OUT FROM BEHIND THE DOOR AND HURRY DOWN THE plane to the back galley. I have to dodge nearly every Greendale kid on board. They're all in the aisles again, riffling through the overhead bins, going through bags. There is stuff everywhere, stacked on empty seats and on the floor between rows. One kid's pulling cash from someone's wallet and stuffing it into his own pockets. Jeanne's actually using her phone to film a video of herself going through baggage and rating the contents on their cool factor. She'd been so hysterical before that it's weird watching her now. It's like she's snapped or something, gone into complete denial about what's going on. I guess a few travel-sized bottles of alcohol will do that to a person.

"Are you serious right now?" I ask.

"I'm a content creator. It's what I do. Besides, Yara's been recording us since we took off, so it's not like I'm the only one." She fluffs her hair and starts talking into the camera again.

"Oh, good. You're back," Kiara says, keeping pace with me down the aisle. "Was your mom like the rest of the adults?"

I nod.

"Damn," she says. "I was hoping she wasn't. We need her. No one's listening anymore."

I glance at the TVs on the seatbacks.

2:18:13.

2:18:12.

2:18:11.

The clocks are still counting down on every TV screen, an insistent reminder that we're running out of time. "We have to drug the old lady and figure out the nearest place to land this plane—soon."

Two boys stumble into the aisle. They're shouting at each other and close to blows. I can smell the alcohol wafting from their mouths.

Kiara stops long enough to smack both of them. "Cut it out, assholes."

The smaller of the two boys rounds on her, but the movement must be too quick because he loses his balance and falls backward into the aisle and just lies there, staring at the ceiling, dazed. The other guy—I'm pretty sure his name is Kevin—doubles over laughing. How many little liquor bottles did they get their hands on? But then I notice an empty full-sized bottle of wine in the seat next to him. There are half a dozen more on the floor nearby.

"They found the wine in the business class galley," Kiara murmurs. "By the time I realized it, every bottle'd been drained dry."

"Does Jack have the Valium mixture ready to administer?" I ask.

She nods. "Yeah. Spencer did most of the work. He's pretty sure we have the right dose."

"Okay, so then let's do it. Now, before things get any worse."

Kiara nods and hurries back up to the front.

I rush the rest of the way to the back galley. I know that I put the old lady's needles into one of the cabinets. Which one? I can't remember.

I slam open one cabinet, then two more. The needles are in the third one. From the moment I pick them up I feel that strange humming vibration in my fingers, the almost electrical current running through them. The symbols have disappeared. They are just two smooth lengths of carved ivory once again. Now that I have them, what do I do with them?

I take out Mom's phone and send a text to Emily.

Now what?

There's no answer.

I stare intently at the needles, but there's no Emily voice inside my head either.

Jack taps my shoulder. "Devon, we have a problem. But we can't talk here." He eyes the bathroom the old lady's locked inside. "Sit with me a second."

He pulls me to an empty row of seats.

I don't want to talk to him right now. I need to concentrate. To hear Emily.

"Remember the air marshal?" he asks in a low voice.

I nod distractedly. We don't have time for this. We need to

drug the old lady, and I need to figure out why my sister's spirit or ghost or whatever wanted me to get the knitting needles.

"He had a gun. I saw it earlier when he restrained the old woman."

"Yeah, I saw it too," I say. "We should get it and put it up with my mom in the crew bunk. Before someone else notices it."

"Listen to me." His voice is urgent. "I already went to get it, so I could do what you're suggesting. Put it somewhere safe. But the holster was empty. Someone got to it first. I just don't know who."

He glances over his shoulder at the rest of the Greendale kids to see if anyone's eavesdropping.

I put a hand on my stomach. It's twisted into such a tight knot it's making me feel sick. The old woman was sitting with the marshal for a while before we moved her. How many kids noticed his gun? Given how clearly visible it was when he restrained the old lady in the aisle, it could literally be any of them. Or it could be the old woman.

My heart beats faster.

"Do you think there's any chance she has it?" I tip my head at the bathroom.

He rakes a hand through his hair. "I mean, yeah, maybe. We didn't exactly pat her down before we locked her in."

I exhale slowly. "So when we go to drug her, if she has it, she could shoot one of us."

"At that close range, she's not going to miss," Jack says. "Which means whoever opens the door could die."

"But if we don't chance it, we can't drug her and break whatever hold she has on us," I say.

He nods. "Yeah, I know."

"Then *everyone* could die."

"What is it? What's going on?" Yara pops up over the seatback in front of us with her phone pointed at Jack, then me.

"Dammit, Yara, stop recording," Jack snaps at her.

"It's important to capture all of this for evidence. I don't get why no one understands this. It's not about me trying to make a film. Jesus, I'm not that cold. And I don't see anyone fussing at Jeanne for recording over there."

"Yara!" Jack barks.

The harshness of his voice makes her flinch. She drops the phone down by her side.

"Okay, okay, I'm sorry." She holds up her hands in surrender.

Of all of us, she's been the calmest. Maybe it's because of the distance her camera provides from the situation—how it makes her more of an observer than the rest of us. Or maybe it's because she's either making or watching horror movies all the time, and she's used to crazy stuff like this. Either way, we could use a clear head right now.

I fill her in on the missing gun.

She whistles softly.

"We're trying to decide what to do," I say.

She presses her lips together and considers what I've said. "There's also a possibility that one of us took it and kept it a secret."

My throat gets tight. "We thought about that, too. But why?"

"I don't know." She shrugs. "Insurance, maybe? I mean, if we're forced to choose a sacrifice, then whoever has the gun gets to be exempt, right? Because they can shoot whoever tries to pick them."

"Or they can make sure that they're the ones who get to choose," I say.

"Or they're planning on using it on the old woman," Jack says. "Taking her out instead of drugging her like we planned."

No matter which scenario it is—the old lady having it or one of us—we're in danger.

"If it's one of us and not her, telling everyone that the gun is missing would be a mistake," I say. "Any chance we'd have of figuring out who it is and safely taking the gun from them would be ruined."

"So what? We act like we don't know? But then how do we safely drug the old lady?" Yara asks.

"I'll go in first," Jack says.

"But if she shoots the second we open the door . . ." I shake my head.

"It's a chance someone's gonna have to take. I'm volunteering to be that someone."

"Why should it be you and not me?" I ask.

"If the adults don't wake up in time, we're going to need help landing this plane," Jack says. "Of all of us, you're the most capable."

"Um, not really. Hearing about how my mom lands a plane and me doing it are two very different things," I argue.

"It's still more knowledge than the rest of us have. You can't open the door. It should be me."

"He's right, so don't try to argue," Yara says quietly.

I stare into Jack's eyes, and he forces a smile. "See?"

Why would he do this? Offer to take such a big risk?

Because he's a good guy.

This time, it's not Emily's voice, it's mine. But that part of me is a liar. It's the part stubbornly holding on to the feelings I had for him last fall. He could also be doing this because he feels guilty. Because he *is* the one who hit Emily and now he's trying to alleviate the guilt he feels—or worse, he wants to make himself look less sacrifice-worthy if it comes down to it.

That's it. It has to be.

I mentally re-armor my heart. I can't trust him. I won't.

Kiara appears, carrying Shazia's tablet and a syringe.

"Ready?"

Andrew, Spencer, Billy, and the others are lined up behind her. The noise and the chaos inside the cabin abruptly cut off. Every kid is staring in our direction.

"Is it time to do it?" Wes appears behind them, his eyes wide.

Everyone looks to me to answer.

"Yes. It's time," I say loudly, feigning more confidence than I feel. "Clear the aisles and get as much stuff back into the overhead bins as you can. Then everybody buckle in." I grab Billy's and Spencer's arms. "Except you two. We might need you."

I rub Emily's locket, hoping somehow it'll bring us luck. God knows we're going to need it.

CHAPTER 15

THE BATHROOM DOOR LOOMS LARGE IN FRONT OF ME. I SQUARE my shoulders and try to muster the courage I'm going to need to get through the next few minutes.

"I'll go in first and make sure she's still cuffed," Jack murmurs, eyeing the back galley from the aisle. "If she is, I'll pull her out of the bathroom."

We lock eyes. I'm going to position myself just outside the door. If she has the gun and she shoots at Jack, the plan is for me to shut the door on her again and lock it. The most she'll be able to shoot is one bullet before the door is closed again. Of course, she could keep shooting, but she'll be doing it blind.

"We'll close ranks behind you." Spencer nods to Billy. "Make sure she stays in the galley."

"We force her into the jump seat and get her harnessed in. Then Jack'll hold her shoulders. You guys get her feet," I say. "Make sure she can't kick or struggle too much."

"Then I inject her with this." Kiara holds up the syringe full of medicine. Her hand is shaking a little. "I tried to get the dosage right . . . but I'm not sure. I mean, Spencer crushed the Valium into as fine a powder as he could, but if there are any pieces too large to pass through her veins, she could have a pulmonary embolism. We could kill her."

"What's she saying?" Rebecca calls from halfway down the plane. She refuses to get any closer to the bathroom and the old lady. I can't say I blame her. Also, it's better that she can't hear what we're planning. She doesn't want us to do this in the first place.

"Nothing. We're just going over things." I keep my voice as steady and calm as I can manage even though I feel like I have a flock of birds fluttering around inside my chest.

"How long before the drug takes effect?" Spencer asks.

Kiara shakes her head. "I'm not sure. Could be up to a half hour. Probably less, though. I mean, she should definitely be mentally impaired before then—enough to break any psychic connection she's got with us."

"If we're right, and this is some form of mass mind control, then once the sedative takes effect, the other passengers should start waking up. And the plane shouldn't lose any altitude," I say. "Because she's only making us think she's got control of the plane. There's no way she can be managing it for real, not from all the way back here. It's on autopilot."

"And if we're wrong?" Billy asks.

"I don't know. I guess we'll have no choice but to give her what she wants," I admit.

"You really believe she won't kill us for trying this? For disobeying her?" Billy asks. He steals a glance at Jeanne and Mai, concern etched into the lines around his mouth and across his forehead.

"She wouldn't be asking us for a body to possess if she didn't want to survive," I say. "She's using the threat of crashing the plane to scare us into doing what she wants, but I doubt she'll actually go through with it. Because she would die too. If any of that supernatural creature stuff is true, the only way she can possess someone new is by having that body chosen for her. She said so herself. So, if we agree to do that, she'll keep the plane in the air and get it on the ground safely just to save herself. But none of that is even rational or remotely realistic, right? It's got to be mind control."

"Okay, so let's do it." Jack claps his hands and heads for the bathroom door.

I get it. This waiting is enough to drive a person mad.

Yara moves so she can record him opening the door.

I wriggle past them both and get into position against the wall beside the bathroom.

We fall silent and listen.

The old lady's humming stops.

I imagine her on the other side of the door, head cocked, listening for us too, and my skin feels like every inch is covered with bugs. I rub at my arms to try to get rid of the crawling sensation, but I can't.

Jack puts a hand on the door latch. "Count of three. One. Two."

On three, he yanks open the door.

I brace myself for the gunshot, but it doesn't come.

Instead, a wave of fetid air rolls out of the bathroom. It smells like raw meat left out in the sun too long, gamey and rotten. I put a hand over my mouth and nose to try to block the smell. Kiara gags.

The old lady is calmly seated on the toilet—same as she was when we locked her in—her legs pressed together demurely, her still-cuffed hands resting on her lap. But otherwise, she is drastically altered. Her hair hangs in limp, greasy chunks around her face. It's thinner, so thin that her scalp shows through in patches of pale pink skin the exact shade of a newborn rat's.

"It's about time. I was starting to get bored," the old woman croaks. Her voice is ragged, phlegmy, and her lips are cracked and bordered by an infected-looking yellow crust. Liver spots speckle her face and arms and hands. She looks like she's aged at least a decade since we locked her in.

"Get up," Jack orders. He grabs hold of one of her arms, his lips curling back in disgust when he makes contact.

She does what he asks, her gaze locked on his face, a smirk playing on her lips as he leads her to the center of the galley.

"Sit down here."

Her knees pop and crack as she settles heavily onto the jump seat. Seeing her this way, she should be less intimidating . . . but somehow, impossibly, she's even more terrifying. It's the erosion of her—it looks like it might be contagious if we get too close.

"Have you made your choice?" she asks.

Instead of answering, Jack clicks the seat harness and then moves to one of her arms to pin it down. Spencer grabs the other.

Carter and Billy crouch to take hold of her feet and press them into the galley floor.

Her gaze flicks from boy to boy, studying them all with a Hannibal Lecter–like grin.

Kiara inches closer, her grip on the syringe so tight that her knuckles are white.

"Yeah, we choose you," Kiara says. Then she pushes up the old woman's cardigan sleeve and inspects the inside of her elbow for a good vein.

The old lady leans her head a little closer to Kiara and sniffs deeply, like she's trying to inhale my friend whole.

"Oh, oh God," Kiara whispers, avoiding the old woman's un-nerving gaze. She brings the syringe closer to the old lady's arm. Her veins are mossy ropes beneath her graying skin. Kiara bites her lip as she decides which one to use.

The old lady whispers something, too low for me to make out. I take a step closer, ears straining. The air inside the galley seems to contract like the oxygen is disappearing. Inside my pocket, the knitting needles begin to vibrate.

Kiara stiffens and her eyes roll back in her head. The hand holding the syringe rotates until the needle is pointed at her own neck.

No.

The old woman's inside her head. Like with Rebecca.

I lunge forward and grab the syringe before Kiara can inject herself with the sedative. Then I turn and plunge it into the old woman's arm, directly into the muscle. It isn't the vein, but it'll still knock her out.

The old bat barely flinches when the needle goes in.

We're eye to eye, so close I can see the tiny red blood vessels in the whites of her eyes. One eye drifts out of position, tilting unnaturally to the left. When it does, something opaque and white emerges out of the corner of her eye, something *alive.* A maggot. It wriggles over her cheek before free-falling into her lap.

I scream and the boys all back up.

Yara drops her phone, then scrambles to pick it up again. The screen is a spiderweb of cracks.

The old woman's pupils dilate and her mouth sags open. A thick rope of drool oozes out her mouth. Her eyelids start fluttering, reminding me of a bird that crashed into our living room window once, the way its broken wing flapped uselessly against the ground. The sedative is working.

Her head droops to her chest.

Within moments, she's out cold.

CHAPTER 16

KIARA SNAPS OUT OF HER DAZE, EYES STREAMING WITH TEARS. She presses her hands to her head.

"Are you okay?" Andrew pushes his way past the other kids into the galley and kneels next to his girlfriend. He lifts her chin and looks searchingly into her eyes.

Kiara shakes her head. "I could feel her in my brain. She made me small inside my own head. I wasn't in control anymore."

It's exactly what I felt at the beginning of the flight. That her description so exactly matches my own sends a shiver of repulsion through me.

"She tried to make you give yourself the shot, but it's okay," Jack explains. "Devon caught your hand and managed to sedate her." The way he's looking at me makes my cheeks heat up, like I did something heroic when I didn't. I was just the closest person to Kiara. No one else could've reached her in time. Besides, reacting—and overreacting—is my default setting.

"What's happening with the passengers? Any change?" I ask the rest of the kids.

Wes hovers over Mr. Lewton. "No, not yet."

Suddenly, the plane shudders. It's nothing big, no more than a shiver really, but then it happens again. Mai moves to one of the windows and stares out into the dark, both her hands pressed to the glass. "We're still level, I think," she says.

"Hey, wait," Wes shouts. His eyelids are twitching. "I think Mr. Lewton's starting to wake up!"

From somewhere up near business class, another passenger moans.

"The flight crew is stirring, too!" Jeanne lets out a squeal of triumph from the front of the plane. "It's working!"

The plane trembles again. Then it dips, not much, just enough to temporarily make my stomach feel floaty. But then it drops again, this time so dramatically my feet lift off the ground.

The old lady's head bobs against her chest. I can't see her eyes because her hair's hanging in her face, but judging by how limp she is, she's still out.

The plane's nose points down then, like God himself lowered it with his hand, and I'm swept off my feet.

Every person not buckled in—me, Jack, Kiara, Yara, Spencer, Carter, Billy, and Andrew—are thrown from the galley area toward the front of the plane. I reach out, desperate to grab onto a seat, anything to stop myself, but I'm tumbling too fast.

Screams erupt all over the plane.

Alarms begin chiming through the cabin.

Then the lights go out.

Someone hits me. An elbow or a knee rams into the center of my back. My head connects with something sharp, and I literally see stars.

We got it wrong. No, I got it wrong. The old woman really is supernatural. And we're not flying on autopilot. She has complete control over this plane. Or had, until I knocked her unconscious. Now we're free-falling to our deaths.

I need to get to the cockpit, but between the g-forces and the bodies tumbling into mine, I can't move. I can barely breathe. I stare into the darkness. Somewhere in the depths of the black, a pair of glowing eyes appears and stares back. The old lady.

Impossibly, the sedative's already worn off.

All at once, the plane's nose comes up. The plane levels out.

"She's awake!" I holler at whoever can hear me as I struggle to my feet. The lights strobe on and off, on and off, like they're struggling back to full power.

I peer into the rear galley. The jump seat is empty. The old woman isn't there.

I fight to scramble out from underneath the mass of bodies pinning me down. Greendale seniors are screaming and fighting their way from their seats to the aisle. The narrow space is packed with people. In perfect unison, the adults and little kids drop into unconsciousness again.

"Get as far to the front as you can!" I yell, but even as I say it, I know it's nonsensical. We're on a plane. There's nowhere to run. Nowhere to hide. Still, I press forward with everyone else. My heart is a pair of cymbals crashing away inside my chest. What do we do now?

We manage to squeeze into business class, all of us crammed in shoulder to shoulder. The lights strobe, then go out again.

The cabin gets deathly quiet.

I pull Mom's phone out of my pocket and click the flashlight on. With trembling hands, I sweep it across the dark space in front of me. The light isn't strong enough to reach the back of the plane. I stare into the gloom beyond the flashlight beam and search for any sign of the old woman.

A dozen more phone flashlights click on. Now it's bright enough to see all the way to the galley.

We stare at the back of the plane, breaths held, and wait.

The bathroom door is wide open, swinging back and forth. Back and forth. Slowly at first, but then it starts picking up speed. It goes faster and faster until it's slamming against the doorframe.

Boom!

Boom!

Boom!

After the third slam, it stays shut.

I clutch Emily's locket with one hand and the knitting needles with the other. They jitter against my palm, like they're trying to fly out of my grasp.

An inhuman howl erupts from the galley. Every hair on my body stands on end. Jeanne bursts into tears and clings to Mai.

I peer into the dark.

Still, there's no sign of the old woman. She has to be hiding in the other bathroom or around the corner of the galley, just out of sight.

We wait. Each second that ticks by is an eternity.

"I don't like this," Spencer says in a low voice.

"This is your fault," Rebecca snaps from where she's huddled in the seat to my left. She glares at me. "We should've never put you in charge. I told you we had no choice. Why didn't you listen?" Spittle flies from her mouth as she screams at me. *"Why?"*

There's another howl. I jerk my gaze back in time to see the old woman finally appear. She's on all fours, gripping the ceiling like a bat—or like that girl from *The Exorcist.* Her head is twisted around at an unnatural angle so it's right side up, not upside down like the rest of her body. Her eyes are feral, glowing like a wild animal's. She bares her teeth and growls.

Then she launches herself down the fuselage, scrabbling across the ceiling like a spider, another inhuman howl erupting from her mouth. She closes the distance between us in seconds, and then she's directly over my head, teeth snapping. I duck out of the way as she drops into the front galley.

Everyone is screaming, including me.

People stampede out of business class into economy, desperate to get as far from the old lady as they can. She watches, a grotesque grin stretched across her face. Billy appears behind her. How he got all the way into the front galley is beyond me, but there he is, hefting a coffeepot over his head.

Before I can yell at him to stop, he raises the coffeepot higher and prepares to strike.

The old woman's head swivels around, farther than should be humanly possible—like an owl's—her face monstrous in the dim light.

She growls at Billy. His eyes widen.

He drops the coffeepot and grabs the side of his head.

She's worming her way into his brain. Just like with Rebecca and Kiara.

Billy blinks stupidly. Then he turns toward the cockpit door and braces his hands against it. His head snaps back then forward with violent speed. He slams himself into the cockpit door.

Wham!

Wham!

Wham!

Everyone stops running. They are frozen by horror and fear.

Blood splatters across the door as Billy bangs his head against it. The cabin fills with screams.

Wham!

This time, Billy's body sways, then crumples into a boneless heap on the floor.

A scream dies on my lips. I can't make a sound. I can't move. My body is too panicked to do anything at all.

The old lady's voice reverberates through the cabin.

"Give me what I want, and this will all be over."

She whirls and slips delicately around Billy's bloodied body.

The cockpit door whips open, and she steps inside. Then she tilts her head and glances over her shoulder. Her mouth turns up into a sneer.

Inside my pocket, the knitting needles start vibrating again. They grow hotter and hotter until I can feel them burning my thigh through my jeans.

The old lady holds out her hand and the needles fly from my

pocket and hurtle through the air to her. She snatches them in one clawed hand with the speed of a viper.

"You have one hour left. Choose. Or you die. There will be no more chances."

Then the door slams shut so hard the entire cabin shudders.

HOUR THREE

CHAPTER 17

"ARE YOU HAPPY NOW? DO YOU SEE WHAT YOU DID?" REBECCA gets in my face, eyes wild. "I told you we didn't have a choice. We should've just picked someone and this whole mess would be over, but *no,* you don't listen to anyone but yourself. You decided what the truth was. How many people's lives are you gonna put at risk before you figure out that you don't have all the answers—or any answers at all? If we'd selected a sacrifice already, no one else would've gotten hurt." She puts a hand to her ruined mouth. "I lost *teeth.* Billy could be dead all because of you. We should've never put you in charge." Her voice rings through the entire cabin. It cuts into me like a knife, slicing away bits of my heart.

I've been trying so hard to be more like Emily, but I'm failing epically.

The others stand in stunned silence. No one argues with her. How could they? She's right. I decided to hold off on the sacrifice. I chose denial rather than face the truth of what we have to do.

I can't save anyone. I keep screwing up and people keep getting hurt.

"I'm sorry," I say. "I only wanted to help."

"Yeah, well, from now on, don't," Rebecca snaps.

Kiara maneuvers delicately past me to Billy. He hasn't moved since he fell. She presses her fingers to his neck to check his pulse.

"Is he dead?" Spencer rushes to her side. He tries to get down on his knees beside Billy, but judging from the grimace on his face, his injury won't let him.

Kiara shakes her head. "He's got a pulse."

Spencer's fists clench and unclench. "What do we do? Tell me what to do."

"Help me move him onto his back so I can see how badly he's hurt." Kiara motions for Spencer to position himself across from her and, together, they turn him over.

Every kid on the plane gasps in unison. Billy's face is a mask of blood. His nose is completely caved in. Jeanne takes one look at him and buries her head in her best friend's chest. Mai just stands there, frozen, her gaze locked on Billy, an anguished look on her face.

Kiara sits back on her heels. Her eyes are shiny with tears.

"I can't do much for his nose other than to bandage it. And he probably has a concussion."

Billy moans and Kiara's eyes light up.

"Okay, good. At least he's coming around. Jack, can you get the Valium? If he's in a lot of pain, we might need to give him one." Kiara chews on her lip. "But I don't know. If he's concussed, is that a good idea? He can't fall asleep if he is. Hey, bring the flight attendant's tablet too so we can see if there's anything in there about treating head injuries. God, I would *kill* for some internet access right now."

I watch my sister's best friend effortlessly take control and the sick feeling in my stomach grows. I should've never let them pick me.

Jack brings Shazia's tablet and the Valium to Kiara and then comes to stand by me.

"You okay?" he asks.

"I'm fine." It's a lie. I haven't been fine since last Halloween and especially not now. But it doesn't matter. Making sure Billy lives matters. Getting us safely to the ground matters.

God, this is all such a mess. I didn't want to do what the old lady asked because I couldn't stomach the thought of losing someone else. But my stubborn need to believe that she was somehow playing a mind trick on us and couldn't make good on her threats put Rebecca and Kiara and Billy at risk. For nothing. We'll still have to choose someone for her to possess. I didn't make anything better. I made everything worse.

I take hold of my sister's locket and squeeze it until my palm hurts. I fooled myself into thinking I could become more like her. But there is no distance far enough for me to outrun myself.

"Devon?" Jack's expression is full of concern as he studies my face. His arms twitch at his sides. I don't have to read his mind to see how tempted he is to put his arms around me.

Because I am just as tempted to let him, to hide my face against his chest the way Jeanne did to Mai. More proof that my first instinct is to choose denial. This stubborn pull I feel to him must be severed. I deserve to feel all this discomfort and pain. To sit with it alone.

"Go help Kiara. She needs you." I turn away and slump into one of the business class seats and put a hand over my eyes so I don't have to see everyone staring at me. No, *glaring.* Choosing someone to sacrifice will probably be easy for them. I'm the obvious choice, aren't I? I might as well offer myself up now. Except I want to survive this night the same as everyone else, even if I've screwed things up. Maybe it's selfish, but it's how I feel.

Jack stubbornly ignores my attempt to get him to go away and sits down next to me.

"This isn't your fault."

I open my mouth to argue, but he holds a hand up to stop me.

"Hear me out. You were trying to save everyone. We had to at least explore the chance that it was possible. Otherwise, how can we live with this? Rebecca's scared. But it's easier for her to show anger than fear. You were an obvious target."

He puts a hand over mine. His palm is warm. Comforting. I want to believe what he's saying, but I can't. I pull my hand away.

Jack's obviously hurt, but he keeps talking.

"You're courageous, you know that? I mean, you're not always right. But you're trying to do the right thing."

I shake my head. "You're not seeing me clearly. I didn't want what the old woman was saying to be true. Every time someone tries to force me into something, I balk, and it's gotten people hurt. My sister. Rebecca. Billy. I run away from hard stuff, Jack. I always have."

"I don't believe that," he says. "You didn't run away from confronting me." He swallows hard. "And even though you're wrong about what you think I did, having you do that helped me stop drinking. I never want to cause anyone that much pain. Especially not you."

My insides are literally at war while he talks. Part of me is starting to believe he's telling the truth, but the other, angrier part of me can't. Because if it's not him . . . I might never find Emily's killer. And I can live with a lot of things, but not that.

My anguish must be obvious because Jack puts a little space between us and clears his throat. "There's something else we need to talk about." He glances around to see if anyone sitting nearby is listening. "Some of the Valium's missing now. I counted the pills before. There were ten in the prescription bottle. We used four on the old lady. But now there's only two. We're missing the other four."

So now we've got a missing gun and missing meds.

Super.

"What is somebody going to do with four pills other than get high?" I ask.

"If they grind them up and mix them with water like we did earlier, they've got a pretty powerful sedative. It didn't work on the old lady, but on a regular human? It could make that person really sick. They might die."

This makes the front of my skull throb. I rub my temples. The old lady is dangerous enough, but now there is one person on this plane stealing away items to possibly use against us in order to save themself. Maybe more than one. Our chances of making it through this alive keep dwindling.

"Is he bothering you?" Carter asks. He moves into the row in front of us and peers over the seat at me.

"I was checking to make sure she was okay, that's all," Jack says before I can answer. He puts a little more space between us anyway, like having Carter scrutinizing him is making him feel self-conscious.

"That true?" Carter asks me, ignoring Jack.

I'm too overwhelmed with the gravity of what's happening to do anything other than nod.

"Make room." Yara pushes Carter over one seat so she can squeeze into the row with him. "You okay?"

"I wish people would stop asking me that." I sigh.

"Listen. There's something I need to talk to you about. All of you." Yara glances pointedly at the three of us as if to emphasize this. "And it's going to sound crazy, but hear me out before you judge me, okay?"

I gape at her. "We're on a plane on Friday the thirteenth with an evil creature masquerading as a busted-up old lady with mind-control powers who can crawl across the ceiling like a scary-ass spider and wants to possess one of us, and you think *anything* you want to talk about could possibly sound crazy next to that?"

Yara tilts her head in a nonverbal "Good point" kind of way and holds up her phone. "So, um, I have this app that I down-loaded for a short film I was working on about a haunted house."

"Yara, just cut to the point," I urge.

"Yeah, okay," she says, her lips twitching into a self-conscious smile. It's weird seeing her like this, so unsure of how we'll react.

She's always so confident. "It's for detecting energy. I started using it on the old lady after she revealed what she really is. I told everyone I was recording what was happening—and I was sometimes—but mostly I was using the app. And, well, some weird stuff showed up."

She rotates her phone so we can see. "It's supposed to detect supernatural energy. You know, like ghosts. They appear as sort of outlines made of different colors—almost like auras or something. In the past when I used it on set for my horror shorts, we'd be lucky to get, like, a partial energy impression. But with the old woman, it's different. . . . See for yourself. I took screenshots. Here's the first one."

The old lady is sitting in the back of the plane next to the air marshal. Surrounding her is a full-body halo with several colors swirling around inside it. It's mostly deep purple and black with a little bit of gray mixed in.

"I thought it was fake at first. I mean, these ghost apps are mainly for fun, something to freak out thirteen-year-olds at sleepovers, right? But I kept trying it on her and taking pictures. And there was always that cloud. Except the colors started changing. Picture that first photo in your mind, yeah? Now look at this one. I took it when you were getting ready to sedate her."

Yara swipes to the next photo. The old woman is in the jump seat, grinning down at Kiara who is midcrouch with the syringe pointed at her arm. The cloud of energy surrounding her is dispersed so that a tendril of it touches Kiara's forehead. I feel a shiver of alarm run through me. It's actual evidence of the old lady infiltrating Kiara's brain. This is what it looks like. I think back to the times earlier in the flight when I could've sworn I felt her trying to claw her way into my brain.

Was that cloud touching me like that? Were there tendrils connecting all our brains to hers when she made it seem like the plane was crashing? I rub my temples and grimace. When I look at the picture again, I can't help noticing something else that's significant. The cloud is dimmer than it was in the other photo. All the colors are there, but their vibrancy is waning. And there are new colors, spots of yellow the exact shade of pus. They are nothing more than tiny blobs speckling the halo cloud, but . . .

"The cloud looks infected," I murmur.

Yara nods vigorously. "That's exactly what I thought!"

She flips to the next photo.

"And this one was taken . . . well, you know, just a few minutes ago."

I stare at the screen. The old lady is on the ceiling, caught mid-crawl, her eyes glowing a greenish white. The pus spots are bigger and there are more of them.

"Now look at this one after we've all been screaming and panicking." Yara swipes to a new photo. In it you can see Greendale seniors in the background. Rebecca, Jeanne, Andrew, and Mai along with others. All of them are terrified out of their minds. Seeing their expressions, I feel my own terror from that moment all over again. But then I study the cloud. The purples and blacks have intensified again. There is the same amount of infected-looking spots, but they've lost their vibrancy.

Yara leans in closer.

"I've been thinking. It doesn't make sense why the old lady let herself stay handcuffed. I mean, she obviously could've gotten free anytime she wanted. We know that now. So why waste an entire hour letting us think we might be able to get out of doing what she asks, patiently waiting until we're more than halfway through this flight to really reveal herself? When arguably she could've forced us into choosing whenever?"

"I have no idea. Why?" Carter asks.

"Can I see those again?" I ask.

Yara hands her phone over.

I go through the photos one more time.

"Her power," I say. "It ebbs and flows, doesn't it? Every time she uses it—like when she made us all think the plane was crashing—those yellow spots increase. When she makes us scared, she regains some power."

"Because she's feeding off our fear," Yara says excitedly. "She let us put her in the bathroom because she needed time to recover. And while we were out here debating what to do, she was sucking in our terror like some kind of psychic vampire."

"So that's why she went into the cockpit just now," I say. "Counteracting the sedative and making Billy hurt himself cost her energy."

Jack shakes his head. "And while we're arguing over who to sacrifice, she'll be feeding on our emotions. Regaining strength. Dammit."

Yara grips the seatback. "If we could get into the cockpit—"

"We can't," I say. "We'd need the door code from one of the flight crew."

"But we could come up with a plan for when she comes back out," Carter says. "I mean, we'll have to go through the motions and act like we're choosing someone to sacrifice to her, but the whole time we can be formulating our next attack."

"No," I say so forcefully that several kids sitting nearby stop talking and stare at me.

I lower my voice. "She can get inside our heads. Any plan we come up with, she'll know and she'll punish one of us again. And her punishments get worse each time. Next time, someone could die, and we'd still have to offer up a sacrifice for her to take. If we choose one person, only that kid loses their life. If we fight, it'll be more. It might be all of us—just like she said. I'm not willing to take that risk anymore."

The others fall silent and stare at me.

"I'm done trying to be a hero," I say. "And you should be too."

CHAPTER 18

"EVERYONE, IF I CAN HAVE YOUR ATTENTION. PLEASE."

I look over Carter's head to where Rebecca is standing in the front galley—in the exact spot where I was earlier when I took charge and gave my little speech.

"What is she up to?" Yara murmurs.

Jack makes a face. "If I had to guess? She's probably seizing the moment and trying to take over. I mean, we *are* running out of time."

We all glance at the TVs.

1:56:07.

1:56:06.

1:56:05.

Jack clears his throat. "We have to figure out who to sacrifice. You know she's going to want to take control of that." He turns to me. "You should go up there too."

"No, it's fine. Let her," I say. I'm relieved that it's her up there and not me. I don't want to be in charge of this part.

"We have to choose someone to surrender to the old lady," Rebecca says. "Now, we could make it random and draw straws or put names in a hat or something, but I don't think that's fair or logical."

"So how do you suggest we pick, then?" Kiara asks. She's managed to maneuver Billy into one of the business class seats. He's obviously hurting, but he's awake and relatively aware, and that's pretty good. Kiara's helping him hold one of the galley towels to his nose to help staunch the bleeding. Spencer hovers nearby. It's enough to make me cry, seeing how upset he is. The two of them have been best friends since kindergarten. When one of them hurts, the other one is always there. It's more than I had with Emily before she died.

"Billy is exempt," Spencer tells Rebecca. "He nearly died trying to stop the old bat. He deserves to be one of the survivors."

"Fair enough," Rebecca says. "Billy isn't a candidate. But this feeds into what I want to discuss. I think the first thing we need to do is narrow down the list of possible candidates. Whoever we choose shouldn't be someone like Billy."

"What are you trying to say?" Jack asks. He clenches his jaw as he waits for her to answer.

"I'm saying we should come up with some criteria to base our decision on. Stuff like who gets good grades, does volunteer work, has a unique skill. Try to figure out which of us brings more to the table, so to speak. Then exempt those people and choose from the ones left, kids who haven't really contributed in any meaningful way, who slack off, or have possibly committed crimes. Or drink too much and then drive themselves home from parties."

She stares unabashedly at Jack and then at me as if waiting for me to offer him up on behalf of my sister. Like everyone else on the plane, she knows I accused him of killing Emily. An hour after I'd done it, nearly half the school knew. Several of Jack's neighbors have Greendale kids in their families and are nosy as hell.

Jack turns from her to me. His gaze is a weighted thing, pressing down on me. Part of me wants to stick up for him. He's been nothing but helpful since we boarded the plane. Heroic, even.

But the other part of me, the angry part, still isn't convinced. All of that could be an act. I mean, if he hit Emily while driving drunk, he'd go to jail. For a long time. His life would effectively end. If he were cowardly enough to leave her lying there alone in the dark by the side of the road, he's capable of doing anything to save himself. Just because he's being nice doesn't make him innocent.

I've let too much time pass between Rebecca's jab at Jack and my nonexistent answer. Which makes everything I've just been thinking obvious, doesn't it?

Jack rakes a hand through his hair. Then he gets up and goes to stand next to Spencer.

"I don't do that anymore," Jack says loudly enough for everyone to hear.

"We don't have time for this," Rebecca snaps.

"Are you serious?" Yara gapes. "About using grades as a gauge? You really want to base the decision of whether or not someone gets permanently possessed on *academics*?" Her lip curls up in disgust.

"It shows someone's smart and a hard worker, so yeah." Rebecca folds her arms across her chest.

"And by that measure you won't get picked," Kiara points out.

Rebecca shoots her a look. "So? Neither would you. Why are you challenging me on this? Besides, grades were only *one* of the things I mentioned. Charity work was another. Special skills." She's repeating herself, so clearly she's already exhausted all the criteria she thinks should count. "Which means your *precious* boyfriend would make the cut too."

"I can't believe we're actually talking about this." Andrew's voice is ragged, tinged with disgust. But he's not objecting, exactly. It's more like he's making an observation—like he isn't so much in disbelief as some sort of terrified resignation. Of course, Rebecca's right. Given his stellar record of charitable work, he's low on the list of candidates for sure—no matter what metrics we use.

Rebecca winces. "Someone has to make us. And since the rest of you are too cowardly to do it, I will. Being a true leader means facing the hard decisions head-on." She looks pointedly at me.

My cheeks burn. I channel Emily and try to remain diplomatic, but inside, I'm fuming. I want to tell her off, but she's right. I can't be in charge of this, not when I have so much to feel guilty about. I can't decide the standards we use because *I'm* hiding things. If any of them knew what happened between Emily and me Halloween night . . . Well, they'd agree I have no business leading this discussion.

"She's right." Jeanne leaves her seat next to Billy and walks to the front to stand shoulder to shoulder with Rebecca. "We have to pick someone. Why shouldn't it be the least successful or deserving of us?"

"Jeanne!" Billy's voice is muffled, probably because his nose is still bleeding under the bandages. He stares at his girlfriend like he's seeing her for the very first time.

Jeanne lifts her chin defiantly. "I'm not going to pick a straw or put my name in a hat. I'm cocaptain of the lacrosse team. I have over one hundred thousand followers on social media. I'm on the honor roll, and I volunteer at the homeless shelter by my house every Thanksgiving."

"This is insane," Jack murmurs.

I look around the cabin at the other Greendale students. What's really nuts is how many of them seem to be seriously considering what Rebecca and Jeanne are saying. I know we have to sacrifice someone, but are they really using social media followers as evidence of their goodness? It's sick.

"You realize that all the people on this trip meet at least one of the criteria you just mentioned, right?" Carter pipes up.

"Well, then we decide who meets the most." Jeanne narrows her eyes at Carter.

"And if there aren't any obvious candidates?" Yara asks. "If all of us are pretty equal in our supposed goodness, what then?"

"That's not possible," Rebecca says confidently, glancing at Jack again. "There are some definite standout candidates already."

Jack's face is pale. I look away quickly.

If he killed my sister, I agree with Rebecca. He should be the one. If only there were some way to know for certain.

There is a crackle of static as the PA system comes on.

A moment later, the old lady starts to speak.

"Good evening, Greendale seniors. We are currently cruising at thirty-eight thousand feet and on course to land on time at Denver International," she says brightly.

Her voice is modulated like a podcaster's. The contradiction between it and the voice she used just before she locked herself into the cockpit is deeply unsettling. I guess now that she knows we're going to give her what she wants, she's having a little fun at our expense.

"Due to the enormity of the decision you have to make and the extremely limited time you have to make it, I've decided to aid you in coming to a consensus. Young Rebecca has exactly the right idea on where to start: worthiness. Which of you is as good as you claim to be? Who among you deserves to be sacrificed? It's a tricky thing to figure out. People hide their true selves so well, don't they? So why don't we shine a light into the shadows each of you harbor? See what sins we can expose? Since Rebecca so courageously volunteered to lead you from now on, we'll start with her."

Eyes widening, Rebecca turns to the cockpit door. "Wait, what?"

"Even good girls do bad things sometimes," the old woman says.

"Not me. I haven't done anything wrong," Rebecca argues.

"Are you certain?" the old lady's voice loses its pleasant lilt.

Rebecca's eyes fill with tears. One of her hands comes up to cup her cheek as if her mouth is starting to pain her again. Is the old woman in her head again, whispering like before? What is she telling her?

"I am a good person," she insists, but there is doubt in her voice.

"Direct your attention to the TV screens and take a seat," the old lady orders. The menace is back in her tone. All at once an image of her gruesome face pops into my head—judging by the gasps of everyone around me, she's in their heads as well. "The show is about to begin."

Kids are frozen in place, gaping at the cockpit door.

Suddenly, I can feel the old lady prying at my brain again. Trying to get in. I grab hold of Emily's locket and try to imagine a thick wall around my thoughts.

The countdown clocks on all the TV screens disappear and are replaced by a blizzard of static.

"No, wait," Rebecca cries.

The old lady doesn't answer—at least not out loud.

"Stop, get out of my head," Rebecca suddenly howls. "Quit laughing at me!"

A moment later, I can hear the old lady's laughter too, a sound like nails scratching on a coffin lid. But she's not trying to work her way out of anything, she's trying to work her way *in*. Into my head. Into all our heads. I clench my jaw and try harder to clear my mind. *Walls. High, thick walls,* I silently repeat, but it's not working. She's in my head. She's . . .

LEAVE! It's Emily's voice, not mine, that's silently screaming. She's here, so strongly it's as if I can feel her sitting beside me.

Immediately, the old lady's telepathic hold on my brain loosens and disappears. But she's still messing with everyone else. All around me, my friends have pained, terrorized looks on their faces. What is she doing? What is she trying to make them do?

I flash back to Billy ramming his head over and over. Then I picture everyone else doing it, dozens of kids ramming themselves headfirst into the walls.

Up front, Rebecca is staring at the static-filled screen above her, her body rigid with fear.

"Don't," she begs.

But the PA system has gone silent.

Every kid still standing—except Rebecca—walks to an empty seat in unison and drops like a marionette whose strings have suddenly been cut. The old woman is forcing us to pay attention.

Powerless, we wait for the static on the TV screens to clear.

CHAPTER 19

REBECCA'S FACE FLICKERS INTO VIEW ON-SCREEN. IT'S A CLOSE-up so extreme that I can see the light-gray flecks in her blue eyes, like tiny shards of ice floating in an ocean.

"What is this?" current-moment Rebecca asks, her gaze flitting nervously from the TVs to the cockpit door. "Some kind of trick?"

On-screen Rebecca is throwing darts at a board full of balloons. "Got one!" she cries, bouncing on her toes. In the background are the faint sounds of carnival music.

"That's the fall festival," Yara says. "At school."

It's impossible that we're seeing this. How is the old woman showing us? Is she pulling it directly from Rebecca's mind?

On-screen, Kiara appears opposite Rebecca wearing a Green-dale High Student Government T-shirt. She's behind a counter, manning the balloon dart booth. She stares at on-screen Rebecca with obvious disdain.

"One balloon busted. So what? With those potato fingers no way you can manage it twice."

It's not the nicest comment, but then Kiara and Rebecca have never been friends. They compete for too many of the same things to ever like each other: president of student council, valedictorian, homecoming queen.

"Oh yeah? Watch me." Rebecca aims another dart.

Kiara folds her arms across her chest and leans against the counter. Behind her, the stuffed animals hanging from the ceiling of the carnival booth sway in the breeze.

"Well, go already." Kiara sighs as she examines her fingernails and feigns boredom.

Rebecca presses her lips together and patiently waits for the breeze to die down before she lets her last dart fly. It sinks into the balloon board, narrowly missing a bright-pink balloon.

Kiara makes a face full of fake regret. "Ooh, *bummer.*"

Rebecca dips a hand into her jeans pocket and slaps down some tickets. "Give me three more."

"So I don't get along with Kiara," current-moment Rebecca says. "She always starts stuff—you all see that, right? I was just trying to play a game. I don't see how any of this proves I'm worthy of being the one we sacrifice. The old lady's manipulating us again. Why do you keep targeting me?" She glares at the closed cockpit door.

Kiara shakes her head at the screen. "I don't remember being that mean."

Rebecca snorts. "Of course not. But you always are to me."

"Because *you* are to *me,*" Kiara says.

On-screen Rebecca throws the first dart. A green balloon explodes. Her lips curl into a smirk. She aims the next dart and snags a red balloon.

"One more and I get a prize," Rebecca crows.

Kiara yawns and looks past Rebecca. A slow smile spreads across her face.

"Hey, baby," she says brightly.

Andrew appears. He's carrying a bright-red snow cone. Kiara leans over the counter and kisses his cheek.

On-screen Rebecca stares at them—no, not them . . . at Andrew. For a second, the camera zooms in on her again. An emotion passes over her face—there and gone in a second, but undeniable. Longing. She's looking at Andrew with unabashed longing.

"I'm not—that's not—" Present-moment Rebecca tries to laugh the moment off, but it's too late. We all saw it. Her gaze flicks to Andrew. He looks away. She bites her lip, and then her face hardens. "It's not like I asked him out. Having a crush on someone's boyfriend is not a crime if you don't act on it!" She yells this last bit to the cockpit door.

On-screen, Kiara takes the snow cone from Andrew and gives it a suggestive lick.

"Thanks, baby," she coos at him.

"Ugh. Do you two mind? I'm trying to concentrate," on-screen Rebecca grumbles.

She aims the last dart.

Kiara leans over and offers the snow cone to Andrew, but her hand slips on a bit of moisture on the counter. She stumbles and the snow cone flies out of her hand. The sugary ice lands squarely on Rebecca's chest, across the deep V-neck of her ivory sweater. She cries out as the cold hits her skin and she stumbles. The dart goes off course and misses the board completely. Rebecca's front is splattered with red. It looks like she's been shot.

On-screen Kiara gasps. "I'm so sorry. It was an accident. I didn't mean to."

On-screen Rebecca glares at her.

"Bitch."

"Hey," Andrew says. "It was an accident. Lighten up."

On-screen Rebecca's shivering so hard her teeth chatter. Several kids nearby point and laugh. She lifts her chin, but it's trembling, and her eyes are welling up.

"Like hell it was. But no one cares, do they? Not when it's perfect Kiara. Too charming to ever get what she deserves. I'm sick of it." Rebecca spits the words at Andrew like they have a bad taste.

Present-moment Rebecca wraps her arms around herself. She turns away from Andrew and Kiara so they can't see her face, so none of us can.

"I'm a good person," she says quietly.

Our student council sponsor and currently unconscious chaperone, Mrs. Sicmaszko, appears on-screen next. "Kiara, dear. Sarah's running late. Can you man the booth for another half hour? Please?"

"Absolutely," Kiara says sweetly.

"Perfect. Thank you." Mrs. Sicmaszko beams at her. She shifts the cash box in her arms so it's resting on her hip.

"Mrs. S., I need to talk to you." Rebecca waves a hand to get her attention and gestures to her sweater.

Mrs. Sicmaszko waves back without actually looking in Rebecca's direction. "It'll have to be later, Rebecca," Mrs. Sicmaszko says. "I need to take this cash to the office to be counted and I've got at least five other issues to deal with before I can go home. Carnival nights are always so crazy!"

"Mrs. S! HELP!" A girl comes running for the balloon booth with her hair literally on fire—just a few strands, but the flames are spreading fast.

"See what I mean?" Mrs. Sicmaszko exclaims. "Good lord, Suzie, what happened?"

She sets the cash box on the balloon booth counter, slips out of the cardigan she's wearing, and smothers the flames. Then she hurries off with Suzie to the first-aid tent.

Kiara gives them both one last concerned glance before she greets a trio of freshman girls excitedly waving tickets. Like Mrs. Sicmaszko, she seems to have forgotten Rebecca's still there.

Rebecca fidgets like she's ready to give up and walk away, but then the cash box on the booth's counter catches her eye. She side-eyes Kiara furtively before she grabs the box, ducks into the shadowy area behind the booth, and slips away. Kiara's so preoccupied with the other players she doesn't notice.

The TV goes black and a new image flickers into existence. Rebecca is inside the school beside a row of lockers. She's carrying the cash box under one arm. Glancing furtively around, she sets the box down next to the locker with the class president magnet on it—Kiara's. She works the combination lock with practiced ease and the door pops open. Laughing softly to herself, she puts the cash box inside.

"I knew it was you!" present-moment Kiara yells from her seat. She stands up, seemingly ready to charge into the aisle. "How did you get my locker combination?"

"I work in the office, remember? They have everyone's on file." Rebecca bites her lip and averts her eyes from the screen. "Okay, so that was stupid, what I did. But you deserved it."

"I deserved it? Because I said you had potato fingers? The second they noticed the cash box was missing, I got called in for questioning!" Kiara shouts. "Do you have any idea how humiliating it was when they did a locker search and found it in mine? The only thing that kept me from getting suspended—or worse—was my perfect disciplinary record." She says this last bit with obvious pride.

"That and your parents saving your ass by threatening to sue the school if they did," Rebecca grumbles. "Perfect Kiara. Someone's always there to bail you out."

"Because I didn't do anything wrong!" Kiara shouts. "I've had to deal with this crap *for months* all because you're jealous of Andrew and me? Get a grip."

"I didn't do it because of him. I did it because you are always such a jerk!" Rebecca shouts back. "It's not like you didn't deserve a little heat. All those times you made fun of me, or rolled your eyes, or talked about me behind my back. I'm sick of it. Perfect Kiara."

"Stop calling me perfect!" Kiara yells.

"So I planted a little stolen money in your locker!" Rebecca snaps. "No one died. And you never got suspended. You're on probation. Big deal. Count it as penance for all your other sins. I don't care what you or anyone else thinks. I'm not going down for this."

Face twisted with rage, Rebecca jams her hand into her pocket. At first, I think she's digging for a tissue to wipe her eyes, but instead she pulls out a gun.

Jack and I lock eyes.

The air marshal's gun.

She must have taken it when we put her on guard duty after Spencer went to the bathroom.

She gets into a firing stance and aims it at each of us. "I've already suffered my share tonight. Being forced to knock out my own tooth is atonement enough for my so-called sin. I don't want to shoot anyone, but I will if I have to. And I'm a good shot. Been going with my dad to the range since I was twelve. So don't try me."

Then she lifts her foot and donkey-kicks the cockpit door. "Show someone else's secret sin. Because we're done with mine."

"Oh, I will," the old lady replies. "The in-flight entertainment is only just beginning."

CHAPTER 20

THE TV SCREEN FLIPS TO THE COUNTDOWN CLOCK AGAIN.

1:38:12.

1:38:11.

1:38:10.

The tension in the air is thicker than Jell-O. I'm literally on the edge of my seat, clutching my stomach. Whose sin is the old lady going to reveal next?

In the galley, Rebecca paces like a trapped animal, the hand holding the gun tensed. Seeing it—the cold metal reality—has my heart racing. What happens if she panics and accidentally shoots? The bullets in air marshal guns aren't supposed to be able to puncture through the cabin, but what if this one can? And where exactly do you hide from a gun on an airplane? There is no place . . . except maybe the crew bunk, but only a few of us could manage to get up there safely. It would mean leaving the rest of the Greendale kids here with her—a different sort of sacrifice, one even worse than the kind the old lady's asking for.

"She's a ticking time bomb," Jack mutters. "We have to get that gun."

Yara turns and peers at us through the crack between the seats. "The gun and these videos are going to make everybody crazy. But it proves my theory, yeah? The old lady's sowing all this chaos, then feeding on our emotions."

I imagine her hunkered down inside the cockpit, head pressed to the door, eagerly inhaling our fear and panic.

When the TV screens blaze to life again, I flinch hard enough that my teeth clack together. Wes screams, fully panicked. And other kids lean close to their TVs, expressions tight and uncertain. Judging from the tension building inside this cabin, most of us are hiding sins and no one wants theirs exposed.

An image sharpens into focus on-screen. It's a meticulously manicured backyard with a pool.

Oh, God. Jeanne's place.

The Halloween party was there.

Is this video going to show my sin?

But then I get a better look at the trees around the yard—how green and lush they are. The giant planters bordering the pool deck are overflowing with lavender. It isn't from fall; it's last spring or summer, maybe. I exhale slowly and my galloping heart quiets. This one isn't mine.

The footage zooms in on a girl passed out on one of the white loungers, clad in a fluffy white bathrobe. Her bare feet hang over the edge of the chair. On the side table next to her is a trio of Solo cups. There are more sprinkled around the cement next to the pool and a beer keg is propped precariously next to a table set up for beer pong. It only takes one glimpse of her long brown curls to figure out who the girl is.

Jeanne.

"Oh, come on!" Jeanne bursts out of her seat. "Seriously? I haven't done anything. My parents know I throw parties at our house. *Everyone* knows. Yeah, I get a little too drunk sometimes, but so does nearly everyone on this plane. I'm not keeping any secrets." Jeanne glances at Mai for support, but Mai's too busy staring at her own TV so intently it's possible she didn't hear one word Jeanne said.

Once again, it's night. I guess maybe it's the best time for hiding secrets—in the dark. Steam rises off the pool, creates a low-lying fog around the lounge chair legs. I half-expect zombies to shamble into view, it's so eerie looking.

Suddenly, Billy surfaces from under the water. Lazily treading water, he slicks his hair back from his face. Then he glances over at Jeanne, who's still out cold on the chair before abruptly turning in the water toward something—or someone—off camera. He grins as he moves in a circle, obviously tracking their approach.

Mai appears with a blanket on her arm. She makes her way to Jeanne's lounge chair and gently shakes her best friend. Jeanne remains boneless, her body barely moving.

Mai unfolds the blanket and gently drapes it across her.

Back on the plane, Jeanne reaches out and hugs her best friend, but Mai is strangely stiff, her eyes wide and alarmed.

On-screen Mai walks over to the edge of the pool. Billy swims toward her, cutting smoothly through the water. She lowers herself to a seated position on the edge of the deck and Billy stops beside her. It's obvious they're talking, but too quietly to be heard.

"Shut it off," Billy murmurs from his seat. They're the first words he's spoken in a while. His face is battered and swollen, especially his nose, but his eyes are more alert than they've been since he hit his head—alarmed, like Mai's.

Jeanne glances over her seat at him and then at Mai before resolutely turning back to the screen, her lips pressed tight together, her body ramrod-straight.

Whispers spread throughout the plane cabin.

Mai buries her head in her hands.

On-screen Billy reaches up and runs his fingers down Mai's leg and her head drops back against her shoulders as a smile spreads across her face.

Jeanne makes a wounded noise.

On-screen Mai turns around just long enough to check on a still-unconscious Jeanne before sliding her body into the pool next to Billy. She presses against him.

The kiss that comes next is deep and passionate and familiar. It's painfully clear that this is not the first time it's happened.

The scream that comes out of Jeanne is almost inhuman with rage.

Mai scrambles into the aisle as Jeanne launches herself at her.

"How could you do this?" she yells.

Mai opens her mouth, but before she can explain, Jeanne slaps her as hard as she can.

"How could you?" Jeanne gets in Mai's face, forces her to meet her gaze.

"Hey, hey." Billy tries to climb out of his seat, but his balance is off.

Jeanne turns on him.

"I TRUSTED YOU!" Her screams morph into gasping sobs.

"I'm so sorry," Mai murmurs.

"Wow, seriously?" Rebecca looks Mai up and down, her nose wrinkled in disgust. She's aiming the gun at Mai, but in a casual way, like she doesn't even realize she's doing it.

"Cut it out," Yara says, but there's no real threat in her voice. How can there be when Rebecca has the gun?

"Why?" Jeanne yells so loudly half the kids in the cabin flinch.

Mai stares miserably at the floor.

"It just happened. Neither of us planned it."

"No. Uh-uh. Not good enough." Jeanne folds her arms across her chest.

"I liked him first. But you probably don't remember, right?" Mai looks up then, a glimmer of defiance in her eyes. "That day in the cafeteria when we first saw him. I pointed him out to you. Said I had a crush on him, remember? And what did you do?"

Jeanne glares at her. "I don't know."

"You walked up and introduced yourself to him, smiling that flirty smile you do when you want a guy's attention."

Jeanne's expression is all innocence.

"I talked to him *for you.* I was trying to help you out. It's not my fault he was interested in me."

Mai makes a disgusted noise.

"You could've said no when he asked you out. A week later you were a couple. You flaunted him in front of my face every chance you got. All that hair flipping and the way you touched his arm. 'Billy, you're too much, *stop.*'"

Mai perfectly imitates Jeanne's musical voice, the coy expression she uses that makes guys slobber over her. The girl does know how to turn on the charm, and there is absolutely zero chance that she's not aware of it.

"But you should've called her on it then instead of going behind her back with Billy. I mean, grow a pair of lady balls, Mai," Kiara tells her, exasperated. "Don't blame your cheating on the person who was cheated on."

Mai's cheeks redden.

Billy clears his throat. "I kissed her. That first night when things started between us. I kissed her first. And I knew it was a bad idea. I just didn't care. I guess that makes me awful, right? But it was pretty much over between Jeanne and me anyway. We were never going to last."

Spencer gets out of his seat and goes to Jeanne. He wraps her in his arms and glares at Billy.

"You're an ass," he snaps. "I've been talking to you about Mai for a solid month and you never told me."

"I promised Mai I wouldn't tell anyone. Not even you."

Spencer hugs Jeanne harder and shakes his head at Billy.

"I nominate them," Jeanne says into Spencer's chest. "Both of them. I don't care if Billy's hurt. He deserves to be back in the running."

There are widespread murmurs of agreement from the other kids.

Billy groans.

"*Come on,* you aren't seriously considering us? For cheating? This isn't the Dark Ages. It's not a hangable offense."

"I don't care!" Jeanne shouts. "I nominate you both."

"I second her nomination," Wes says eagerly. "We should just vote on which of them to choose right now. Then we won't have to watch any more videos."

There is a chorus of agreement from nearly half the Greendale kids. "I vote Mai!" someone shouts.

Mai starts to sob.

"Come here." Rebecca waves her gun, motioning at Billy and Mai to head into the galley with her. She's bold, confident in her own safety.

When they don't move, Wes grabs Mai and another kid hauls Billy to his feet.

"Please, no." Mai tries to wrestle her arm out of Wes's grip, but he's holding on too tight.

"Vote! Vote! Vote!" people begin to chant.

But then the TV starts to flicker again, a clear sign that a secret's about to be revealed.

"Wait. Let's see what's next," Rebecca says, obviously enjoying herself now that she's clearly not going to be voted as the sacrifice.

"No, let's vote," Wes insists, jerking on Mai's arm for emphasis.

Rebecca levels the gun at his chest.

"I said we're waiting."

Wes's already pale face goes ghostly.

"Okay, sorry," he murmurs.

Rebecca's mouth curves into a pleased smile. Everyone's paying attention to her now.

"You better hope whatever sins that get revealed next are worse than yours," she tells Billy and Mai. "Because otherwise, one of you is going to become the old lady's new body."

CHAPTER 21

WHEN THE TV FLICKERS TO LIFE AGAIN, THE VIDEO FOOTAGE IS different from the other two times. The camera is shooting inside a car from the driver's point of view. But who are they? The steering wheel is center frame and beyond it is an oily black eel of road slithering out past the headlights, only partially visible because it's night and there aren't any streetlights.

Carter and Yara look back at me, frowns on both their faces.

"What is this?" I ask out loud.

Don't watch.

The words are Emily's. She's back inside my head again, so suddenly present that she's all around me.

Don't watch.

She repeats herself, louder this time.

"Emily?"

Goose bumps break out along my arms, and the hairs on my

neck stand on end. My sister's presence is an electric current in the air.

Don't. Watch.

Her words are so clear it brings tears to my eyes.

"Why not?" I ask.

"Who are you talking to?" Carter asks, his voice shaky.

"I keep hearing my sister," I whisper.

Jack turns in his seat now too. He looks worried, which makes my stomach drop. Is this really happening or am I just going crazy?

"How?" he asks.

"I don't know," I admit.

"What's she saying?" Yara's hand is trembling so badly she can barely keep her phone aimed on me.

"She says I shouldn't watch." I nod toward the screen, then try to look away, but now I'm curious. Why can't I watch?

An army of tall pine trees stands sentinel beside the road as the car speeds along. They are silent and imposing against the moonless sky. Loud music blasts through the car's interior, some vintage rock ballad I recognize but can't remember the title to.

The PA system crackles to life.

"Young Devon, this is for you."

The old lady's voice feels as if it's enveloping my head. Yara takes out her phone and aims it at me. Her mouth drops open.

"Oh, wow," she whispers, awed. "She's trying to get inside your head. I can see it. I can actually see it." Yara moves her phone from my face upward toward the ceiling. "Those tendrils like with Kiara—they're coming from the speakers above you."

I don't need to see what she's seeing to know she's right. I *feel* them.

Don't watch.

Emily again, but her presence is waning, as if the old lady has taken over, pushed her out. I try to fight her off, but it's too late. Those tendrils are already worming their way into my scalp, down to my brain. Suddenly, my body is no longer under my control. She's with me in my head. My hands drop to my lap. My face turns to the TV screen. I can't make my eyes shut. She's going to force me to watch.

My heart gallops out of control, and my head throbs with the sudden rush of blood through my veins. I try to take a breath, but it's hard. The old lady's presence is all over me, thick and oppressive.

I can't see anything but the car and the road and the trees on-screen and then it's like I'm in the video, behind the wheel, driving. I can feel the steering wheel against my palm, the gas pedal under my foot. I can hear the steady roar of the engine.

The dash glows softly. The speedometer climbs as the driver picks up speed.

60 mph.

65 mph.

70 mph.

I try to look into the rearview mirror, but I don't have a reflection. There's just the back seat. A tiny stuffed version of the Greendale High bulldog mascot dangles from the mirror, ticking back and forth like a metronome. And there's a book on the passenger seat. Its cover gleams softly from the moonlight coming through the window.

"What is this?" I can't turn my head to see who's talking, but I recognize Rebecca's voice. Only it's muted, far away from me.

The car takes a turn a little too fast and judders off the road briefly before the driver course-corrects. The road opens back up, giving way to a pristine stretch of asphalt. There's a sudden break in the trees where a two-story colonial brick house sits back on a wide lawn sliced down the middle by a long, winding driveway. It is twin columns with lanterns flickering on top.

My mouth goes dry.

I know this house.

It's less than a mile from Jeanne's place. There are jack-o'-lanterns clustered around the mailbox. My mouth goes dry and my stomach flips.

It can't be.

Carter must recognize it too because he whips around and peers over his seat at me. I can see him in my periphery, but I can't turn my head.

"Do you think this is from Halloween night?" he asks softly.

Yara gasps.

I can only nod because the old woman's stolen my ability to speak.

This is the car that killed Emily.

The driver is the person who killed my sister. This is why the old lady's showing me this. But she isn't letting me see who it is. She's playing another game, taunting me with the one thing I've spent the past four months trying to find out.

My insides are crawling, but I can't move. I want the camera to switch its point of view. I need to see who's driving the car.

But instead, the video cuts off.

No! I silently scream. I swear I can hear her laughter echoing inside my brain before her grip on me loosens, then abruptly disappears.

"Put it back on. PUT IT BACK ON!" I yell the moment I can speak again.

But the screen stays dark.

Jack crouches into the aisle beside me.

"Are you all right?"

I shake my head.

The old lady knows. She knows.

"I want to see the rest!" I shout. "Show me!"

But there is only silence from the cockpit.

"Why is she doing this? What does she want from me?" I grab the sides of my head with my hands.

Jack gently squeezes my knee.

"Was it you?" I ask, pulling away, my whole body shuddering with rage.

Jack recoils like he's been stung.

"That car wasn't mine."

"You can't tell that for sure from the video," I say.

"What's it going to take for you to believe me when I tell you it wasn't me?" he asks, his cheeks flushing.

"Proof," I say. "I need to see the killer with my own eyes." I rub the top of my head where it felt like the old lady's tendrils were attached.

And even if it means letting her inside my mind again to do it, I will.

CHAPTER 22

THE NEXT TIME THE TVS POWER BACK ON, IT'S WES'S FACE FILL-ing up the screen.

"Oh, hell. No, no, no." Wes starts freaking out the second he sees himself. "I knew it. I freakin' knew it." He jumps out of his seat and makes a run for the first-class bathroom, his eyes bugging out of his head.

Rebecca blocks his way and aims the gun at him.

"You're going to stay. And you're going to watch."

"Please," he begs, falling to his knees at Rebecca's feet. "Don't make me."

"If I had to watch mine, you're going to watch yours." Rebecca keeps the gun trained on his head.

"Dude, calm down. How bad can it possibly be? You're lit-erally a Boy Scout, for crap's sake." Carter's eyes are focused on Rebecca's gun as he says it.

"Yeah, man. Just do what she says." Spencer frowns.

Wes flinches.

Rebecca's lips turn up a little. She's got all the power. Even the most physically intimidating kid in our class is daunted by her right now. It's obviously going to her head.

Wes lets out a noise that's half-sob, half-sigh. But instead of going back to his seat, he slumps in the aisle, brings his knees up to his chest, and hugs them close. He stares at the TV screen on the wall above Rebecca.

On-screen Wes is wearing black jeans and a black hoodie with a pair of combat boots. There's a black knit cap perched on top of his head. It's the opposite of his usual style, which consists entirely of preppy shirts and khaki pants.

He's standing in a dimly lit hallway at our school. Prom posters paper the walls. The darkness of his clothes and the hallway is in stark contrast to his paperwhite skin. He looks practically ghostly standing there.

"The footage is from last spring." Kiara touches her TV screen. "See? The posters are *Great Gatsby*–themed."

It's hard to concentrate on anything other than Wes. The look on his face . . . it's strange. Normally he's sort of expressionless. Calm to a fault. It makes him easy to overlook. Bland Wes. Studious and mousy. Completely harmless and forgettable. But now on-screen he's a tightly coiled spring. His face is all hard angles steeped in the shadows. He exudes barely maintained rage.

From somewhere close by, there is the sound of a crowd cheering. Judging from the trophy case clearly visible behind Wes, he's in the hallway at the back of the gym near the doors that lead out of the locker rooms. He glances around. Satisfied he's alone, he yanks on the edge of his knit cap and pulls it down over his face. It's not a cap at all, but a ski mask.

"You look like a bank robber. Kind of scary," Kiara murmurs, eyeing current-moment Wes.

I know exactly what she's feeling. It's like we're seeing a total stranger, not Wes at all.

Spencer makes a strangled noise. His hand goes down to touch his knee. Every muscle in his body has gone completely rigid. Watching him, it hits me what we're about to see.

On-screen Wes reaches behind himself and pulls a short black metal rod out of the waistband of his pants as one of the locker-room doors opens. Spencer strides into frame wearing his wrestling singlet and earbuds. He's looking at the ground, nodding in time to whatever music he's listening to, so he's too distracted to notice Wes standing there, watching him. He's in the zone, working himself up for his match.

Wes breaks into a run.

Spencer doesn't see him until it's too late.

The steel baton is already arcing downward.

Whap!

We all flinch when it connects with Spencer's knee.

His leg bows backward at an unnatural angle. Spencer collapses, screaming.

On-screen Wes turns almost elegantly and strikes him again, same leg, but the upper thigh this time. Spencer's whole body jumps on impact. Two more violent strikes and then on-screen

Wes is running for the exit door at the end of the hallway that leads to the parking lot. He's fast, sure-footed. This was a planned attack and he pulled it off perfectly.

The camera zooms in on Spencer's anguished face and holds there while Spencer screams and screams and screams. Then the TVs go dark.

"You little piece of shit!" Spencer roars.

He yanks Wes up from the floor and punches him: one, two, three times in quick succession. Blood sprays from Wes's nose and mouth.

"I lost everything because of you! My scholarship to Penn State. Ever being able to wrestle again." Spencer grinds out the words and then throws Wes to the ground.

"You deserved it." Wes spits blood onto the carpet and then wipes his mouth, smearing more blood across his check. His eyes are wild, not scared anymore, enraged. He's a cornered animal, baring all its teeth. "He bullied me. All of you knew it. The teachers knew it. Hell, my own parents knew it. But instead of stopping him, people made excuses. Can't suspend the school's big champion and risk losing donors."

"Come on! It was stupid stuff. Shoving you into lockers. Pantsing you at the senior class bonfire. Nothing close to what you did. You *ruined* me!" Spencer's shouting so intensely, spittle flies from his mouth.

Jeanne snickers at the mention of the pantsing and then quickly claps a hand over her mouth.

"You have no idea what it feels like to have everyone treat you like the punch line of a joke every day of your life for *six years*!"

Wes yells back just as intensely. "My father said I needed to stand up to you and show you I wasn't weak and then you'd leave me alone." Wes angrily wipes at his tear-filled eyes. "So that's what I did. And it worked, didn't it? You were too injured to notice me anymore. I'm not sorry. You ruined yourself by being an asshole."

Spencer starts to lunge at him again, but Jack steps between the two of them and holds him back.

"Don't do it. It's what the old lady wants," I say to Spencer. "She's feeding off our anger and fear. You're only going to make her stronger."

And then the PA system crackles to life again and the old lady makes a *tsk*-ing sound. "It doesn't matter what I want. It's what you need, Spencer. *Justice.* This boy stole your future. He murdered the man you were supposed to be. And what are you now? Broken and in so much pain that you've become a drug addict."

Spencer's face hardens.

"So pitiful you've been stealing the pain medication on this plane. Hoarding it for yourself."

"SHUT UP!" Spencer hollers, the cords on his neck straining.

"Make it even. Take from him what he took from you," the old lady urges.

Wes crab-walks backward to put space between him and Spencer. All the bravado he had a second ago is quickly being replaced by terror the longer the old lady talks.

I step out into the aisle. If we can't talk him down, Spencer is going to kill Wes.

"Don't let her inside your head," I whisper, grabbing hold of Spencer's arm.

Spencer's face is contorted by rage. "I want to kill him."

I'm not sure if the old woman's already gotten her claws into his brain or if this is really him talking, but does it matter? I believe him. He is so close to murdering the kid. And of course, it's what the old woman wants, the perfect meal to make her grow stronger. But no way am I going to let her coerce us into taking any extra lives. It's unbearable enough having to choose someone to sacrifice.

"Ending him won't fix your knee," Jack says softly. "Your life doesn't have to be ruined. But if you do this, it will be."

"We can't let her divide us." I put a hand on Spencer's arm. "We need to stick together and stay calm. Decide who to choose as a group. No one goes rogue, okay? That's how we survive this."

Spencer's hands are still balled into tight fists, but his shoulders relax just a little. Reluctantly, he nods. "Fine, but he's got my vote for the sacrifice."

"That's fair, man," Andrew murmurs wearily. He's sweating and literally on the edge of his seat. Another few minutes and he might totally lose it. As hard as it is for all of us to endure this, it's obviously wreaking the most havoc on him. The boy who spends his entire life trying to save others is having to help choose someone to sentence to death.

"He's my vote, too," Billy says, grimly. "Rebecca planted some fundraising money and Mai and I cheated, but assault and battery is on another level. He's the obvious choice."

"Agreed," Kiara says from her place next to Andrew. There are deep hollows under her eyes. This flight is clearly taking its toll on her too.

The old lady's laugh filters out of the speakers and the hairs on the back of my neck stand up when I realize no one else seems to be reacting to it—like they can't actually hear her anymore. Her presence is . . . close to me. She's working her way inside my head again.

If they vote now, you will never figure out who your sister's killer is, she whispers inside my brain.

I shouldn't listen. I just got done telling Spencer not to let her inside *his* head, and now I'm ignoring my own advice. But she knows who Emily's killer is. If we're going to sacrifice anyone, it has to be them.

"Wait!" I shout. "The secrets are getting progressively worse, right?"

Yara's got her phone trained on me. Her eyes flick from the screen to me and narrow. She knows the old lady's got her tendrils in me, but I don't care.

"If we vote before she's done showing us all of them, then we might let someone more deserving than Wes off the hook."

"Like who?" Jeanne asks. "Who could possibly have done something worse?"

"Emily's killer," I tell her. "The old lady showed footage before of the car that hit my sister. Why would she do that unless the person who hit her is on this plane?" I try to scan everyone's faces fast so I can study their reactions, but there are too many kids and it's impossible to distinguish regular terror from the guilt-induced kind. Whoever Emily's killer is has become good at hiding.

"She's right," Rebecca says. "If we're going to be fair about this, we need to see everyone's secrets."

"Easy for you to say," a boy a few rows over pipes up. "You're already out of the running."

Rebecca raises the gun in the air. "I was never in the running. Not really. Not while I have this. And if I say we're going to watch all the secrets, then we are." She turns and nods at me like we're suddenly a team, which turns my stomach, but whatever. I can pretend to team up with her if it means finding the person who hit Emily.

I vowed to get justice for my sister no matter what it takes. And that's what I'm going to do.

CHAPTER 23

I STARE SO HARD AT THE SCREEN THAT MY HEAD STARTS TO HURT. I'm back in the car on the road by my house. I'm watching the video playing on all the TVs, in the killer's POV again. But this time, the old woman isn't forcing me to. I want to see this. I need to know what happened, no matter how awful it is. I owe it to Emily.

The footage picks up where it left off, with the car zooming past the colonial house and toward another tree-flanked patch of pitch-dark road. That same rock ballad is playing, heading into the guitar-solo bit. The noise sets my teeth on edge. I'm so tied up in knots I might jump out of my skin any second.

The car winds through the dark, trees blurring past the windows because it's going so fast. The song crescendos into the final chorus. We're getting closer and closer to my house, to Emily.

I don't realize that I've started grinding my teeth until my jaw starts to ache. Emily's already dead. This video isn't in real time, and yet my entire soul is screaming inside me, sounding an alarm.

Stop this. Save her.

Except I can't.

I study the inside of the car for a second time, scrutinize every detail for a clue that might give away who's driving. There is an iPhone lying faceup on the center console, but its screen is dark, save for the faint reflection of the dashboard lights on the end closest to the gear shift.

When it suddenly glows and starts to vibrate, I'm watching the screen so intently that I cry out.

Damn!

The phone-screen image is the default, nothing personal at all. Too far away for me to see all the app icons. Someone's calling the driver, but the number comes up as possible spam. The driver's hand appears. It's gloved.

I make a strangled noise. This was October—Halloween. It makes sense that the driver would be wearing gloves, especially when I notice the temperature on the car's digital display. Twenty degrees. I'd almost forgotten how cold it was that night.

The driver reaches for the phone, but accidentally knocks it off the console and into the passenger footwell instead. It lands faceup. The driver exhales noisily and leans over, one arm reaching across, fingers stretching toward the phone.

I watch the screen carefully, study the blue-jacketed sleeve attached to the gloved hand for any clues to the driver's identity. After three desperate grabs, the driver finally manages to pick up the phone. The camera jerks back to the windshield as the driver straightens up.

Someone is on the road ahead. It's as if they materialized into existence. The driver inhales sharply at the same time I do.

Suddenly, the camera speed slows way down. The old woman obviously doesn't want us to miss a second of what's about to happen. This moment should be over in a blink, almost too fast to see, but slowed down, every detail is in sharp relief, suspended for seconds at a time.

My sister's sleek blond hair covers her face at first, so I can't see her eyes, but of course it's her. I'd know my twin anywhere. Her identity is clear in the subtle curve of her shoulders and the way she holds her hands like a dancer, always graceful and poised. She's halfway across the road, midstride, her pale skin gleaming like polished ivory in the harsh glare of the headlights.

Emily. I say her name inside my head over and over like a plea, a prayer. But it isn't going to help. It's much too late. My heart shatters into a million pieces all over again, the way it did when I first found out she was dead.

The tires screech as the driver stomps on the brakes. The speed drops, but not fast enough. The car starts to fishtail. Left then right, then left again.

Emily's head jerks up. The video is so clear that I can even make out the car's headlights reflected in her eyes. Her lips part. Surprise and terror wash over her face.

The blood in my veins goes icy and goose bumps rise along my arms.

Yara makes a strangled noise and covers her face.

Jack is sitting beside me, but when he takes my hand I'm still surprised. His grip is solid and real.

"Don't look," he whispers.

His words are muffled by the roar of blood in my ears. I can't take my eyes off my sister's face. She looms larger and larger on-screen as the car careens toward her. There are tear tracks glistening on both her cheeks, the remnants of the hurt I caused earlier that night. Her mouth opens and she screams, but between the rock music—made sinister now that it's in slow motion—and the squealing brakes, I can't hear it.

I scream too. My voice blends with my sister's and the brakes and the music, a ghastly quartet.

The car hits Emily and the book on the passenger seat flies at the windshield as she comes up over the hood. Then, in nearly the same spot that the book hits the glass, Emily's head does too.

The sound. Oh, God, the sound.

The heavy thud her body makes guts me. I wrap my arms around my stomach like somehow I'll be able to hold myself together. Spidery veins of shattering glass spread across the windshield, obscuring my view. Emily is a blur of black winter coat and blond hair, half shadow, half wraith, seen through a mosaic of broken glass and blood. There and gone in an instant.

Emily is quiet now, but I am still screaming.

I can't seem to stop.

The car skids toward the grass on the side of the road and the video footage fades to black.

When I found out how Emily died, I conjured in my head a

million times what the accident must've been like. But nothing prepared me for seeing it play out for real. The plane is holding altitude, but I am free-falling. The world I've been living in has been ripped away and there is nothing but space, black and deep and infinite, stretching wide like a mouth, eager to swallow me whole.

I hold myself tighter. *Get a grip, Devon.* I can't lose it right now. Not here. I bite my lip hard enough to draw blood, counting on the pain to shake me back to the present.

"Dammit!" I cry.

Yara gets out of her seat and crouches next to me. "Devon, are you okay?" Her voice is shaky, unnerved, and there are tears streaming down her face.

"No. I want to see who's in the car."

The rage that's been keeping me company since Emily died has gone from a little ember inside my stomach to a roaring fire, consuming all my patience and more than a little of my sanity. The old woman knows who killed Emily, but instead of showing us, she's drawing it out, torturing me.

Keep control.

Emily's voice echoes through my head again. But I don't really care about staying in control or whether or not my anger is feeding *that thing* in the cockpit. All I want is to figure out who killed my sister and make them pay.

"Who is it?" I stand up. "One of you killed Emily. Who?"

Every Greendale kid on board stares wide-eyed at me. No one speaks. No one moves.

Rebecca clears her throat. "Come on, Devon. No one's stupid enough to confess." She isn't glaring at me this time. If anything, there's pity in her eyes. And if these stupid airplane seats weren't bolted to the floor, I'd pick one up and throw it at her. I don't want pity. I want answers.

"I'm going to figure out who you are!" I shout.

"Sit down, Devon." Rebecca gestures to my seat with the gun. Her eyes have gone slightly blank, and I can tell it's not her, not completely, not anymore. It's the old lady's voice I hear when she opens her mouth again. "We have another video to watch."

CHAPTER 24

I'M EXPECTING TO SEE THE CAR AGAIN, FOR THE CAMERA TO PAN inside it and finally reveal who the driver is. But that is not the image that pops up on-screen.

Jack is kissing me.

It's the night of the Halloween party.

He's James Bond, dressed in a sleek black suit with a fake gun holstered to his hip. I'm a pretty decent Joan Jett in a leather jacket and striped pants with a spiky black wig—the Queen of Rock 'n' Roll herself.

Jack has my face cradled in both of his hands. He's pressed against me, kissing me with an urgency that makes current me's face heat up.

No. No. No.

I've been so wrapped up in the footage of the car hitting my sister that I stopped worrying the old lady would show my sin.

But this is it. The moment I've been dreading since the footage started playing in the first place.

Every kid on the plane turns to look at Jack and me, but I keep my gaze locked on the screen. I can't face their stares—or Jack's.

The camera pans out a bit so it's clear we're in a bedroom. On-screen me lies back against the mattress and pulls Jack on top of me. He leans on one elbow and gently removes my black wig. I shake out my blond hair.

Someone whistles softly.

The really messed up thing about this moment is that even now, watching it all go down, I get the same deep belly-pull of longing I had that night. My body can't seem to stop wanting him . . . or, more precisely, my heart can't. It's not smart or rational, and it's loathsome considering what happened after this, but I can't make it go away. I can't even try to channel my sister in this moment. I am still the old me at my core. I guess no matter how hard I try, I always will be.

You see? You can't be redeemed. It's a waste trying so hard to. Once an apple goes rotten, it's no good anymore.

The old lady's claws dig into my brain again. Her voice is in my ear, the words like insects burrowing in, making a home inside my head.

On-screen, there is a knock at the door. Three hard raps.

"Devon? Are you in there?"

The door swings open and Emily strides into the room with one hand over her eyes. She's got her winter coat slung over her other arm and no real costume, just her regular clothes.

"Can you leave my sister and me alone, please?" she asks on-screen Jack. Her lips press together tightly as she waits, one foot tapping impatiently. "Now?"

I want to crawl under my airplane seat. On-screen, Jack and I are still entangled, and my shirt is pulled up, so my bra is showing. Jack is worse. He clumsily tries to hide the bulge in the front of his jeans as he works his way off the bed. Then he sways and nearly falls as he stumbles to the door, too drunk to say anything to Emily or to on-screen me as he goes.

I spent most of last fall trying to orchestrate a time when he and I could be alone. I've never wanted a boy as much as I wanted Jack, and that night—for a moment—it finally felt like he was seeing me the same way I saw him. He wanted me. And I was elated . . . until my sister showed up.

Emily shuts the door behind him and leans against it. She pinches her nose with her fingers the way she always did when she was getting a headache. It made her look like Mom—older than me. I always resented that, her innate maturity, because it made me feel stupid and small.

"Really, Devon? Him?"

On-screen me puts my hands behind my head and stretches out across the bed. I want to smack the smirk right off my own dumb face. It's an act. I was trying to piss her off. Not only did she ruin my moment with Jack, but she made me seem foolish for wanting it—for wanting him—in the first place

"What? He's hot," on-screen me says with an edge of defiance in my voice.

Current-moment me cringes. A few weeks later, I was in Jack's driveway taking pictures of the damage to his car and accusing him of murdering my sister.

Current-moment Jack stares at the floor, his face and ears flushed. He seems as embarrassed as I am. He obviously regrets that night too.

Somewhere in the cabin, someone snickers.

"He's wasted more than he's sober, Devon. How can you be so obsessed with such a total loser?"

Cringing, Carter steals a glance at current-moment Jack.

"She's right. I was. Back then. Before," he murmurs.

But I can barely pay attention to what he says next because this is the moment. This is when things go horribly, awfully wrong.

"God, you're such a buzzkill." On-screen me groans loudly. "Loosen up for once in your life, why don't you? I know you're a total nun, but that doesn't mean the rest of us have to be."

Emily hugs her jacket to her chest.

"Mom and Dad know you've been skipping school. They called and told me to find you and bring you home. I guess they tried your phone first, but you were, um, too busy to notice."

On-screen me bolts upright on the bed.

"You told them?"

Emily opens her mouth to protest, but on-screen me hurls a pillow at her face.

"Dammit, Emily. Can't you ever have my back? Why do you always have to be such an uptight bitch?"

Back on the plane, Yara inhales sharply and I cringe. She hasn't even heard the worst of it yet.

My sister's eyes go hard.

"I'm not going to help you self-destruct. One more unexcused absence and you'll fail this year. Mom and Dad were going to find out eventually. Better that they did before you're a high-school dropout. Because we both know if you have to repeat the year, you won't go back. The minute anything gets inconvenient or hard, you bail."

"That's bull. I don't bail on hard things. I bail on *pointless* things. I didn't skip school to mess around. I skipped for band practice. We've got that big competition coming up next weekend. There'll be music execs there. It's our shot to break out. So yeah, it took precedent over school. *Nothing* I'm learning in my classes is going to help me make it as a musician. Winning this competition might." On-screen me is so sure of herself that it hurts to watch.

Emily stares at on-screen me, a look of utter incredulity on her face.

"You aren't allowed to do it anymore. Mom and Dad said you're grounded. You're supposed to give me the car keys so I can drive us both home, and then you'll only be able to go from there to school every day. That's it."

On-screen me's face contorts with rage.

"Oh, hell no. I'm not going to miss it. I could lose my place in the band permanently. The guys'll have to replace me or forfeit our spot."

"Well, you should've thought about that before you started skipping school." Emily glares at me. "You made a deal with Mom and Dad. You could be in the band as long as you passed all your classes. You're the one who flaked on your promise. Not them."

"God, you sound just like them, you know that? Good, sweet Emily. So mature. Never does *anything* wrong."

"Give me the keys, Devon." Emily sighs heavily.

On-screen me sneers at her.

"No."

"Give me the keys," she demands.

On-screen me gets off the bed and folds my arms defiantly.

"There's no way I'm going home with you."

Emily laughs humorlessly.

"Yeah, okay. Sure. Come on, give me the keys, Devon."

She holds out her hand, but when on-screen me just stares at her open palm, she snaps.

"You think I want to have to deal with this tonight? I had my own plans, you know. Plans that didn't include taking you home. Plans that were really important to me." Her voice breaks a bit. Hearing it makes my heart squeeze uncomfortably. She's trembling and visibly upset, but on-screen me is too angry to notice.

What was she talking about?

I don't remember her saying any of this that night—or, at least, I wasn't paying close enough attention to notice—but now I'm curious. What was she getting emotional about?

"Not that you care," Emily continues. "You're too wrapped up in yourself to worry about anyone else. I'm so *sick* of you. We're twins and it's crazy how little you really know me. You decided who you thought I was a long time ago, and to you that's who I'll always be, right? I'm just this version of me you've conjured up inside your own stupid head."

"Well, you don't know me either," on-screen me says.

Emily throws up her hands.

"Dammit, Devon. Whatever. Just give me the effing keys."

"You want to go home, you can walk," I say. "I'm not voluntarily going back there so Mom and Dad can make me miss the competition. I'll stay at Carter's."

Emily snorts. "Like his parents won't send you home once Mom and Dad contact them."

"Then I'll stay with the guys. I'm *not* going home. Not until after we win and I get a recording contract. Maybe not ever." On-screen me tilts her chin up and stares down her nose at my sister. "My music's more important than not pissing off Mom and Dad. I won't give up my big break over some missed classes. Screw high school. And screw you for telling on me in the first place."

Emily makes a frustrated noise.

"GIVE ME THE KEYS!"

She launches herself at on-screen me and tries to wriggle a hand into the pocket of my jeans.

"Get off!" on-screen me roars as we start wrestling, each of us grappling desperately for the upper hand.

"Give me the keys. Give me the mother-effing keys." Emily grabs a hunk of my hair and pulls.

On-screen me howls and gives her a forceful shove. She loses her balance and falls backward onto her butt, hard enough that a lamp on a nearby table topples. *Whack!* It lands on the back of her skull before crashing to the floor.

Emily grunts in pain, then grips both sides of her head and screams.

"God! I am so over this crap!"

On-screen me watches her, my chest heaving, one hand patting down the hair she pulled.

"Sometimes I can't stand you." There is venom in her voice.

On-screen me looms over her.

"Yeah? Well, I hate you," I watch myself say. "Every single time I'm having fun you shit all over it."

Emily stands up and angrily wipes at the tears rolling down her cheeks. "Whatever, Devon. Just whatever. You're gonna drop me at home even if you're not going to stay. Everyone left at the party is too drunk to drive. There's no one else I can catch a ride with."

"So?"

Emily blinks.

"It's only like thirty degrees outside and there aren't any Ubers at this hour. Our house is nearly five miles away!"

"So what?" On-screen me has zero pity. It's worse than anger or hurt; it's total indifference. Seeing it, my whole body feels like it's fissuring, about to break into a thousand pieces.

Here it comes.

"You know what?" on-screen me blurts out. "I hope you freeze to death out there. It would make my life a hell of a lot easier if you weren't in it."

On-screen me doesn't wait to see her reaction. I just head for the door, the car keys dangling casually from my fingers. My shoulders straight and stiff and defiant as I head into the hallway past a sloppy-drunk Kiara in a Queen of Hearts costume.

"Have you seen Andrew?" she slurs. Then she spots Emily. "Oh, hey, what's wrong?"

But Emily doesn't answer her. She's crying too hard. Kiara tries to give her a hug, but Emily slips out of her grasp. She grabs a tissue from the bathroom and blows her nose; then she rushes past Kiara, slips into her coat, and disappears down the stairs and out the door just in time to see me back out of the driveway and speed off into the night.

CHAPTER 25

"BRUTAL," REBECCA EXCLAIMS SOFTLY AFTER THE SCREEN FADES
to black and the countdown clock reappears.

1:14:02.

1:14:01.

1:14:00.

I slump in my seat and cover my face with my hands. I think
about the last conversation I had with my sister all the time.
Sometimes the memory feels like an anvil chained to my chest,
suffocating me. The only thing that helps is trying to keep her
alive however I can. It's why I dress like her and try to be like her.
I was wrong about what I said. She wasn't the one who messed
things up. I was. I should've been the one who got hit. No one is
better off without her. Not Mom and Dad. Not any of her friends.
Especially not me.

"That was pretty messed up," Rebecca says. "Wishing her dead
and then leaving her like that. You ever hear about the power of

manifestation? The universe heard what you said and made it true. You're basically a murderer."

"Leave her alone, Rebecca," Jack says, his voice tight with barely contained anger.

Rebecca shakes her head.

"Uh, no way. We have to figure out who to sacrifice. Obviously, the old lady agrees with me on this or else she wouldn't have shown Devon's fight with Emily, right? Right?"

She is pacing the floor, gesturing with the gun. Several kids cringe away from her when she passes, but not Jack. He keeps eye contact and stares her down.

"She wanted to hurt her sister emotionally, not kill her," Jack says.

"Don't," I say.

He turns to me.

"Don't what?" he asks.

"Defend me," I tell him. "I don't deserve it."

I don't drum anymore because I don't deserve it, either. I *should* lose the things I love most. Because Emily lost her life. And maybe this is why I've been so mad at Jack all along. Did I ever really think he killed my sister? Or did I just decide to blame him to keep him at a distance, to keep us apart, so I could punish myself some more?

"You didn't mean it. I know that. We all know that," he says.

"I don't know that," Rebecca argues.

"Shut up already," Spencer barks at her.

Rebecca shivers and then cocks her head to one side. When she opens her mouth to speak, it's the old woman's voice that comes out.

"You can't bring her back, but you can even the score."

A cold chill crawls up my skin.

"If you give me your body." Rebecca's smile is so wide her lips split at the corners. I can see the gap where her tooth was, swollen and angry-looking. The gun shakes as her hand convulses. Somewhere inside herself, Rebecca is trapped, straining to get free, but the old lady's hold is too strong.

"A life for a life. I'll be a better Emily than you are," she says. "Your parents will feel like they never lost her at all. And you can save all your friends. Spare them the guilt voting will bring."

Out of the corner of my eye, I can see the other kids looking my way hopefully. They're willing me to volunteer. This is what the old lady's been driving toward this whole flight. She wants me to be her next body. All I have to do is agree and it ends now. Isn't that the noble thing to do? Isn't this what I really deserve?

The temperature in the plane drops noticeably. Suddenly, I can see my breath, the way I could up in the crew bunk when I was with Mom.

Something tugs the locket around my neck.

DON'T!

"Oh my God," Yara says, training her phone camera on me. "Emily is here. I can see her energy." Yara looks equal parts terrified and amazed. Tears stream down her face. She nudges Carter. "Look at this. Do you see it?"

Carter stares, utterly speechless.

My sister is with me, all around me. So present that my eyes get watery. I can smell her perfume. I grab the locket and grip it tight.

"I'm so sorry for what I said. I was mad and I didn't mean it. Let me do this. Let me save the others," I tell my sister.

Above me, the overhead bins fly open and luggage rains down into the aisle.

Everyone starts to scream.

"I don't think she wants you to sacrifice yourself," Yara murmurs. Her hands shake so badly that she drops her phone. She ducks into her seat to get it, but then stays there, covering her head with her hands. She's scared out of her mind.

Beside her, Carter clears his throat. "Um, actually, she might be mad because of me. Some of this is my fault too."

I lift my gaze to meet his. The moment our eyes lock he totally loses it and bursts out crying. Carter's always been a little sensitive, but even so, this much emotion isn't normal for him. It scares me more than the tossed luggage.

"I've tried to tell you a bunch of times, but something or someone always interrupts our conversations before I can . . . or else I lose my nerve."

"What are you talking about?" I say, and then I remember how Halloween night he was missing from the party. "Tell me you didn't hit her."

"No! It's not that." He wipes angrily at his face. "I'm the snitch. Not Emily. I told your parents that you were skipping school."

"*You* told my parents?"

He nods miserably. "I was worried about you. You were so obsessed with your music. Nothing else seemed to matter anymore. Not school. Not your family. Not me. I believe in you, but you were torpedoing the rest of your life on a maybe, and it wasn't you. Not the Devon I've been best friends with since elementary school." He's talking fast again, all his words are running together. "So it's my fault you were grounded. If I hadn't done that, you and Emily wouldn't have fought. You wouldn't have left her at the party. She wouldn't have died."

I'd be lying if I said part of me wasn't really angry with him. But in this moment, with so many secrets being revealed, and that awful hag hovering behind the cockpit door, it seems petty to be upset. His motives were pure. Born of concern. Just like Emily's.

I won't make the mistake I made with Emily with Carter. I won't blame him. I made my own trouble. I always have. The only person I should be angry with is myself.

"Thank you for caring about me." I grab hold of him and hug him tight. I can feel all the tension in his muscles release. He hugs me back just as hard.

"You should let Jack off the hook now too, Devon," Carter murmurs against my neck. "I don't think he hit Emily. And if you're finally being honest with yourself, neither do you."

"Jack." I untangle myself from Carter. "Where did you go that night? After you left?"

He presses his lips together. "I got in my car and passed out. Jeanne's neighbor woke me up just after dawn because I was blocking his driveway." He shakes his head. "I was still a little wasted, but I drove myself home anyway. It was beyond reckless. Utterly stupid. And I hit my garage door."

"How come you never mentioned there was a witness before?" I ask.

Jack's jaw flexes. "You needed someone to blame. And I guess

I needed to be punished somehow, even if it wasn't my fault. I got in the car and drove drunk. It wasn't even the first time. I didn't hit your sister, but I could have. I went into rehab after I heard she died. It scared me so bad I practically begged my parents to send me. The really messed up thing is that I got this second chance to do better even though I didn't deserve it, and your sister was such a good person and she got killed. It made no sense. So when you thought it might be me, it felt like justice because it hurt so much to have you hate me."

What he's saying makes perfect sense because it's exactly how I feel.

Jeanne clears her throat then. "Hey, I hate to interrupt, but are you going to sacrifice yourself? Because if you aren't, we're running out of time." She gestures to the TV screen, where the countdown clock ticks back the seconds way too fast.

1:07:03.

1:07:02.

1:07:01.

Emily's locket grows cold against my neck. I can't hear her voice, but I think I know what she wants. Why she got so angry. She doesn't want me to sacrifice myself, because she still needs me to figure out who her killer is.

"No. At least not yet," I say.

"We can still vote for you," Wes says. "Right? She told her sister she wished she was dead. She abandoned her. That's worse than what I did."

"No, it's not," Spencer growls. "Sit down and shut up, or I'll shut you up."

Wes's face pales and he slinks back to his seat.

Spencer gives me a grim nod.

"So what now?" he asks.

"The old lady shows us who hit my sister. Then we vote."

"How do you know she'll show you who it really is?" Kiara asks. Her face is swollen with tears. She's been crying a lot. And her voice is strained. I've been so preoccupied with how the last video made me feel, it never occurred to me to check in with my sister's best friend. The last few minutes have obviously damaged her. She can barely look me in the eye. I guess she hates me now. Because of my fight with Emily. Because of what I never told her I said.

"How can we believe anything she shows us?" she asks.

"Because so far every video's shown the truth," I say.

Kiara cries harder and starts shaking her head from side to side.

"No. I don't want to watch any more. I can't take this."

She pushes past me into the front galley and sits with her back against the cabinets, facing away from the TVs. She hugs her knees and begins to rock back and forth, back and forth. Andrew hurries to her side and tries to put his arms around her, but she pushes him away.

Rebecca eyes them and shakes her head.

"See? This is why she was never going to be a good leader," she says more to herself than to anyone else, dabbing at the bloodied corners of her mouth. The old lady isn't in control of her brain anymore, but Rebecca isn't exactly herself either.

"Go on and show us who killed Emily." She taps her gun against the cockpit door. "Let's end this already."

CHAPTER 26

WHEN THE TV SCREENS FLICKER BACK TO LIFE, THE CAMERA IS hovering above a shallow, muddy ditch filled with gravel and dirt. Emily is splayed out across its center, her arms and legs bent at unnatural angles. Blood surrounds her head. Tears slip down her cheeks. She blinks up at the sky, directly into the camera, as if she can see it. Her chest heaves, pumping up and down way too fast. She's panicked. But it's only seconds before it all changes and her mouth goes slack.

The time between breaths gets longer and longer.

I swallow bile. At this exact moment, I was heading to see the guys from my band. I didn't care that I was defying my parents or that I'd left my sister to fend for herself after midnight on Halloween night. Remembering it now, I nearly throw up. My sister was dying, and I was too busy figuratively sticking my middle finger up to her, our parents, and the world to wonder where she was. Or worry how she might get home.

I pull out one of the little paper vomit bags and dry heave into it. Am I strong enough to watch my sister's last moments?

The plane is too small, too close. There is nowhere to run, no way to escape from the revulsion I feel for myself. I fidget in my seat, but I don't look away. It doesn't matter if I can handle this. I have to watch, to experience every awful second. I owe Emily at least this.

On-screen, my sister looks so, so scared.

I reach out and squeeze Jack's hand so hard it must hurt him, but he doesn't pull away. My sister was alone and I am an awful, terrible person. I just want the screen to go black, go black, go black.

Emily exhales one last time. The final bit of warmth inside her body drifts out into the cold night air, a faint cloud there and gone in a blink, her soul disappearing.

There are no words to describe how this makes me feel. So I stay quiet. I hold Jack's hand. I try to remember how to breathe.

Suddenly, the camera zooms out so that it captures Emily from the outer rim of the ditch. There is the sound of footsteps, someone running. Then a sudden quiet as whoever is approaching stops short, feet skidding on the loose gravel. A pair of shoes appears. No, not shoes. Boots. Combat boots with skulls painted on the tops of each one.

My heart skips a beat. I know those boots. I saw them tonight. Right before we took off.

They belong to Yara.

I wrench myself free from Jack's grip and erupt into the aisle.

"It was *you*?" I stare at Yara, this girl who has never seemed like she's hiding anything at all. Who has been by my side through the whole flight, trying to figure things out with me. She killed Emily? I'm so stunned, for a moment I don't know what to do or say.

She raises her hands as if in surrender.

"I found her, but I didn't hit her. It wasn't me," she says. "Please, let me explain."

But I am pain and anger and grief in this moment. Every emotion inside me coalesces into a blinding rage, and all I want to do is strike out. I want her to hurt like my sister hurt. Like I hurt.

"You sat on this plane with me for the past three hours when you were there. YOU WERE THERE!" I yell, my voice cracking under the weight of my emotions. I can't contain them anymore.

I throw myself onto Yara and knock her down into the aisle.

"Why?" I ask over and over. I shake her shoulders so hard, her head bounces off the floor.

"Please. I can explain." Her words come out in fits and starts. There's blood on her lip. She must've bitten it at some point.

STOP! Emily's voice is a scream inside my head this time. A sliver of icy cold slices through my brain. My sister is so, so angry. I stumble backward, away from Yara. Tears course down my cheeks, hot against my skin.

Suddenly, Jack and Carter are beside me. They each take hold of one of my arms.

"That's enough, Devon," Carter says quietly. I wrench out of his grip, my chest heaving. I can't seem to get enough air. Emily is still here and that anger . . . it's almost a tangible thing. But it's not directed at Yara, it's directed only at me. Why? I thought this is what she wanted. For me to discover who killed her.

Jeanne and Rebecca huddle around Yara, blocking her with their bodies.

Rebecca frowns and points her gun at me. "You need to calm down."

Everyone is watching me, eyes wide and horrified. The only sounds are my ragged breathing and the constant hum of the plane's engines.

"Hear her out." Jack's voice is quiet but firm.

"She killed my sister. That's all I need to know," I gasp.

Yara sits up and cradles her stomach with her hands.

"I didn't. I swear. I found her after," she pants. "You have to believe me. I would never, ever hurt Emily."

"Liar!" I yell with enough force to make myself light-headed. I want Jack to let me go. I struggle against him, but he only holds me tighter. I've never been this angry. I want to strike out at him and Yara, at everyone. Again and again until my knuckles are bloodied and my body is spent. I can't deal with this much pain. "If you didn't do it, why didn't you tell me you were there that night? Why did you just leave her in that ditch? Why have you spent all these months covering it up?"

"I DIDN'T KILL EMILY." Yara throws her hands up. "I mean, I don't even have my driver's license. Or a car. Everyone knows I don't drive. Don't I even get a chance to explain?"

LISTEN.

Emily's voice booms inside my head again.

"It doesn't fit, Devon." Carter goes to Yara and puts his hand on her shoulder, and it throws me. If there were any doubt in his mind about her guilt, he wouldn't defend her, not to me. Not after he played a part in my fight with Emily. "I know her well enough to see that. After everything we've been through on this flight, don't you?"

I fold my arms.

"Go ahead," Jack urges. "Explain."

I glare at him.

He locks eyes with me. "You've been wrong before."

Listen.

Emily's voice again, insistent and stubborn.

Yara sniffles.

"I never would've done anything to hurt your sister. We were . . . close. She was supposed to meet me at the Halloween party that night. So when I couldn't find her in the house, I went looking outside." Anguish twists her expression.

"But you weren't even friends," I argue.

Yara inhales deeply.

"Your sister had secrets too." She clenches her jaw so tight for a second that I'm not sure she'll start talking again, but then she does.

"I was one of them."

Sighing, Yara digs a hand into the collar of her shirt and digs out a necklace—no, a locket. Just like Emily's. She holds it up so everyone can see.

I can't make sense of what she's saying. Okay, so over the years

Emily and I drifted apart, but still. Emily was an open book. She was too perfect to have anything to hide. And what does she mean that she was one of Emily's secrets?

Then, all at once, I understand. I hear Emily's voice inside my head, the words she said to me more than once the last few months she was alive.

I can't ever have a crisis of any kind or be nervous or confused or scared or uncertain, because you have more than enough drama brewing for the both of us, Devon.

Was my sister gay? If she were, I would've at least suspected, right? Wouldn't there have been clues? But then I think about how little time I spent with her. Even if there had been, I was hardly around enough to notice them.

"We used to meet up," Yara says, her gaze trained on me. Her chin lifted, defiant. "And yeah, at first it was only because of this project I was doing. A documentary about high achievers for my film class."

I remember this. From last year. Emily mentioned it once or twice, but I tuned her out. It just felt like one more spotlight on her and I resented it like hell.

"I don't know when it changed. It wasn't all at once. We just had fun doing the interviews for the documentary. Then she offered to help me edit the footage. I don't think either of us realized it was more, at least not for a while."

"You're gay?" Carter asks.

Yara shrugs.

"Honestly? I don't know. I'd never been attracted to a girl until Emily. I think for me it's more about the person, not their gender.

What I do know is that she gave me butterflies. Lots of them. And it felt really good." Yara smiles softly, remembering.

"Emily told you she liked you too?" I ask. "But she always dated guys. She never mentioned liking a girl."

"I think it was the same for her. We were mostly just attracted to each other?" She says it like a question, like she isn't sure. "That's why we kept it secret. We didn't want to have to put a label on it. So we were taking things slow."

Yara wipes at her nose again, then stares at the blood on her fingers.

"But I was falling pretty hard for her. And maybe she was too, for me. We were trying to figure out if it was time to go public and what that would mean. We were planning on telling our parents, but she kept stalling because you were ditching school and getting into trouble. She didn't want your parents to have to deal with anything else. We were supposed to talk it over more on Halloween. Maybe tell you first to see how you'd react before we told your parents, but you never really gave us the chance, did you?" There is a trace of bitterness in her voice now.

Her words are a knife thrust straight into my heart. Emily was hiding all of this, and I was so caught up in my own drama that I didn't even notice. How could I not have noticed? I never got to know my twin for who she was. I am a terrible sister. Selfish. Rotten. I say a silent *I'm sorry* to Emily in case she's still with us, but I can't feel her anymore. It's as if she can't manage to stay with me for longer than a few minutes at a time.

"I waited for her at the party. When she didn't come and she wasn't answering her phone, I started walking to your house to figure out what was going on because I didn't have a car and I didn't want to have to explain to anyone else why I wanted to see your sister that late at night. I thought maybe she was changing her mind about us. I didn't even see her on the ground at first. It was pretty dark and I had my phone flashlight aimed toward the road. But then I heard a noise. Like a gasp or something. And suddenly there she was." Her voice breaks and she starts to cry. It's obvious how much she cared for my sister.

Yara wipes at her face and shivers.

"I went to her, but there was nothing I could do." Her eyes are far away, haunted. "We weren't totally ready for people to know about us, and then she was dead. I knew that wasn't how I wanted them to find out. So I got her phone and dialed 911. I told them where she was and hung up. It was the hardest thing I've ever done. Walking away from her." Tears are pouring down her cheeks now, but she doesn't seem to notice. "I hid in the woods until they came. I couldn't stand the thought of leaving her there all alone.

"After, I wanted to tell you a thousand times," Yara tells me. "But you were so angry and then you were so . . . different. You dressed so much like her that I could barely stand to be in the same room with you. It hurt too much. It was like I was losing her all over again every time I saw you. Besides, you've been a total mess. How could I give you something else to handle on top of everything you were already dealing with? It was easy to see how much you blamed yourself. I didn't want to make that worse." She hugs herself, turtles into her sweater as if it's armor. "I had to hide how sad I was from everyone—even my parents. I've been so alone the past few months. But what else could I do?"

In the background, the footage of the hit-and-run is playing on repeat. I was so focused on Yara I hadn't noticed, but now it's all I can see—the horror on Emily's face, her skull cracking against the windshield. The blood. Her broken body.

"Stop it! Stop playing that!" I yell.

My rage has sharpened, become a hard knot inside of me. The old lady tried to trick me into going after Yara, into sacrificing an innocent person. Is Emily's killer even on the plane or is this just a ploy she's using to break me?

Right now, the only person who truly deserves to be attacked is the old woman.

But she's hiding like a rat in a hole.

I rush forward and pound on the cockpit door. Drum an angry beat with both my fists.

"Come out here, coward. Or are you too weak to face me?" I drum harder, a steady, insistent rhythm. "I bet that's it. You're not as powerful as you claim. Why else would you hide?"

The cockpit door rockets open and for the first time since we took off, I can see the pilots slumped in their seats. Except they aren't like the other adults on the plane.

They aren't sleeping.

They're dead.

The fronts of their uniforms are covered in blood. She's stabbed them. Just like Carlos.

I stare, horrified, at the two men, at their eyes, open and unseeing. Behind me, kids start screaming. They've seen the pilots too.

The old woman stands between them, grinning wickedly, her skin literally peeling back from the bone in places: her cheek, her collarbone, her chin. But her eyes are a vivid, radioactive blue, and she's emanating strength and energy despite the decay. She's been feeding off all our grief and anger and guilt and is practically glowing from the meal.

But I'm too angry to care.

It's time to end this.

HOUR FOUR

CHAPTER 27

"WHO KILLED MY SISTER? NO MORE VIDEOS. NO MORE GAMES. Tell me now." Before I can lose my nerve, I grab the old woman's wizened arms and drag her from the cockpit, then slam her against the bathroom door. It rattles in its frame. Her eyes glow brighter on impact. She lowers her head and growls at me.

"Don't! You're only going to piss her off." Rebecca's voice is pure panic. She aims the gun at me, but there's no way she can shoot me without hitting the old woman.

The old lady cackles and somehow I know she's still feeding—on Rebecca's panic and my anger. Her laugh gets harder and harder until it morphs into a cough. A glob of blood-speckled mucus flies out of her mouth and lands on my bottom lip and chin. I flinch then gag. I can't help it.

The *smell*.

My stomach lurches and my grip on her loosens. She takes advantage of the moment and latches onto my arms, drives me backward down the aisle so fast that I stumble and fall. Hard. My lungs compress. I can't breathe.

The old woman drops down onto my chest, pinning me to the floor. Her awful face looms directly over mine. It's all I can see. A long strand of drool drips from her mouth. I turn my head, trying desperately to avoid it.

Her stare is cold and reptilian. This close, it's like I can see the supernatural creature squatting inside the old woman's body. It is enjoying this. All of it.

"Come now. I've shown you everything you need to figure out who it is. You just have to pay better attention."

"Just tell me." I am practically pleading now.

She shakes her head slowly back and forth. "Tsk, tsk, tsk. Where's the fun in that?"

"How can I be sure Emily's killer is really on this plane?"

"You can't. Not unless you let me in. Will you let me in?" She grins, her mouth stretching wide over yellowed, rotted teeth. Something hums inside her mouth. A lot of somethings. Her jaw seems to unhinge and suddenly a cloud of flies comes pouring out. They swarm over my skin, my face, and try to wriggle into my nose and ears. "Be my new body," she says. The words are thick in her mouth, garbled by the insects still writhing inside.

I claw desperately at my skin to get the flies away. Screams erupt throughout the plane as they lift into the air and disperse through the cabin.

"I want you to be the one," the old woman whispers directly into my face, her hot, fetid breath wafting over me in waves. "It would be so easy. You've already given away so much of yourself trying to be like your sister. You're an empty vase, waiting to be filled."

That's why she's taunting me with these videos. With answers she won't reveal unless I give my body to her. "What if I refuse?" I croak.

"Then you have to choose someone else. Let them take the fate you deserve."

"No." A tear slips down my cheek.

"Aw, poor Devon. Always so guilt ridden. Life is made of regret. You survive long enough and sometimes it's all that's left." Her eyes glitter. "And it tastes soooo good." Her tongue darts across her desiccated lips.

Then she leans down and plants a dry kiss right on my lips. I gag so hard bile burns my throat. Then all at once my whole chest goes warm.

Oh, God.

Did she infect me with something when she kissed me? Fear swarms around my insides like the flies.

But when the old woman clambers to her feet, the warmth quickly gives way to wet, and I realize that her bladder must've given way. She just peed on me.

The old woman looks down at the darkened stain on her pants. Her lips curl back in disgust. Her current body is failing fast even as the creature inside grows stronger.

"Oh my God, gross," Yara murmurs. She's holding up her phone, using the app to measure the energy fields. I wonder how infected they look now.

The old woman hurtles down the aisle and back to the cockpit, and the flies follow. Kids scurry out of her way. She stands behind Rebecca and whispers in her ear. Rebecca stiffens, then holds the gun up, aims it toward the cabin.

"Make your choice," she cries.

The TV screens begin flashing insistently and the countdown clock appears again.

00:50:44.

00:50:43.

00:50:42.

The other kids begin to talk all at once. Jeanne yells out Mai's name. Wes shouts that it should be Spencer. A few other kids yell out Wes's name.

I hear my name next. People spill into the aisle and start shoving each other. Things are going to get out of hand soon.

I scramble to my feet and lift my shirt so the wet spot isn't resting on my skin. "Ohmygodohmygodohmygod," I say over and over as I work my way back to my seat. I shouldn't leave when everything's so chaotic, but I can't stand to be in these clothes. I rip off Emily's sweater then the shirt as I go until I'm just in my sports bra. I don't care who sees. I can't have that thing's pee clinging to me like she's marked her territory.

I yank my backpack out from under the seat in front of mine and pull out my sweatshirt, then I head to the bathroom and wash the pee off as best I can with the hand soap and a wad of paper towels. No matter how much I scrub, I can still smell the gamey tang of her urine. I gag so hard my eyes water.

I glance up into the tiny mirror above the sink. My eyes are wide, haunted and wild. My hair is severely disheveled—no longer straight and Emily-smooth. I look a little like the old Devon after a particularly intense drum session. It's hard seeing this version of me again. I've gotten so used to seeing Emily in my reflection. The old lady's right about one thing: I have given myself away, bit by bit, little by little until there doesn't seem to be much of me left. I cram my wet shirt into the trash and examine Emily's sweater. I breathe a sigh of relief. It's urine free. Thank God, because I don't want to have to throw it away—ever. I scrub my hands one more time until my fingers are tingling.

A knock at the door makes me jump.

"It's me," Yara says through the door. "People are straight-up fighting out here. We have to do something."

When I open the door, she hands me a travel-sized bottle of perfume.

"To banish that witch's stank," she says.

A surprised laugh bubbles out of me.

I spray some on my chest.

"Thanks."

"I'm sorry you had to find out about Emily and me the way you did," she says softly.

"I'm sorry I made it impossible for you both to tell me."

"If we get out of this, maybe we can talk sometime," Yara says hopefully.

"I'd like that." I hand her back the perfume. "We better get back up there."

Yara leans into the back galley and grabs a metal tray from the refreshment cart.

"In case we need to whack some heads," she says, walking briskly back up the aisle.

I stop at my seat for a second to grab a ponytail holder and my brush from my backpack so I can corral my out-of-control hair into a quick ponytail. The brochure for the ski resort falls from the front pocket and slides to the floor. I stoop to pick it up—no easy feat considering how narrow the space is between this row and the one in front of it. I'm not sure why I'm bothering except maybe to distract myself from what's going on, even if it's just for a few seconds. The brochure managed to slide all the way under my seat. Sighing, I grab it and sit back on my heels a second and stare at the glossy photos of snow-covered slopes.

The ski trip is like something from another lifetime. It's as if we've been on this plane forever, and yet the clock won't stop racing to zero. I glance at the TV screen on the seatback nearest me. A little less than an hour left until the end of this flight. Except I still don't know who killed Emily. I don't want to choose anyone else. But what choice do I have? I toss the brochure onto the seats. It lands on top of Andrew's journal.

My breath catches in my throat.

With trembling fingers, I move the brochure away and pick up the journal.

Dark brown leather with a bronze clasp.

It feels like I've been punched.

I turn to the TV and it flickers, begins playing the footage of

Emily's hit-and-run again. I wait for the moment of impact even though I know what I'm going to see. I need to be one hundred percent sure.

There.

The book. Dark brown leather. Bronze clasp.

Andrew was driving the car that hit my sister.

Andrew left her on the side of the road to die.

And he's kept it secret all this time.

I mentally sift through every interaction with him that I've had since Emily died. He never looks me in the eyes. He got so sick after the old woman told us she was going to make us choose a sacrifice. He's been so quiet, so utterly uninvolved with everything and everyone. He's been hiding in plain sight.

I open the journal and flip through it, searching for all the November entries. And then there it is, a single entry. Just four words.

What have I done?

"Devon? What's wrong?" Jack is beside me.

I dodge past him.

"ANDREW!" I yell his name at the top of my lungs, with every ounce of energy I have. My body is alive with anger, every nerve on high alert. Adrenaline courses through my veins. I want to hurt him. I want to hurt him so badly.

"What's happening?" Jack asks, jogging to catch up with me as I cover the distance from the back of the plane to the front. The business-class aisle is jammed with kids, everyone yelling and shouting at each other. Someone throws a punch and clips my ear.

"ANDREW!" I shout again, my temples throbbing.

I shove people out of my way, duck and weave until I'm through the throng.

The old woman is waiting near the cockpit.

I'd forgotten all about her. There's a dark stain along the crotch of her pants and blood pools along the underside of her neck beneath the skin. Her body looks past death, but that thing inside her is giving off energy in waves, so strong now that the air feels thicker somehow.

"Where is he?" I demand as I make my way up the aisle.

She doesn't answer, just watches me with those awful glowing eyes of hers.

"What happened?" Yara asks.

"Andrew killed Emily. It's his journal in that car." I hold up the leather book. "He basically confesses in here."

"See for yourself." I throw the journal to Jack.

"Where is he?" I demand.

"I don't know. He and Kiara were in the front galley a few minutes ago. But I don't see them now." Jeanne's voice trails off.

She's right. Kiara and Andrew aren't in business class or the galley.

I check both bathrooms. The first one is empty. When I open the second one, Rebecca's unconscious inside.

I shake her roughly.

"Devon, ease up. She's hurt," Carter says from behind me.

Rebecca groans.

"What happened?" I need her to answer. *Now.*

Rebecca rubs her head. "I don't know. I was standing in the

galley, and something hit the back of my head. Everything went black." She starts to cry when she pulls her fingers away from her scalp and they come back red.

"Rebecca, where's your gun?" Carter asks.

She looks around the narrow bathroom, frowning. "I—I don't know."

Andrew and Kiara.

They took her gun.

Rebecca's eyes widen as she realizes her leverage over all of us is gone. She shrinks back against the bathroom wall, tears streaming down her cheeks.

I turn back to the cabin. The cockpit door is gaping open. No one but the two dead pilots are inside. Andrew couldn't have gone to the back of the plane without passing Yara or me. So where?

I turn to the old lady. Her lips curl back into a self-satisfied smirk. The last few minutes have been chaos. Everything is falling apart—exactly as she's orchestrated it.

Our time is up and the one person who most deserves to be sacrificed has disappeared. No, not disappeared. He's hiding. But I've checked the bathrooms. Where else?

The hairs rise on the back of my neck.

There's only one other place to hide on this plane.

The crew bunk.

Kiara knew about it. She watched me go in and was waiting outside when I came back down.

She and Andrew are hiding up there with a gun. Where my mother is: unconscious, helpless, an unwitting hostage. If they hurt her, I swear . . .

I make a sound deep inside my throat. I can't lose someone else I love.

Frantic, I scan the galley for anything I can use as a weapon. There is only the ice hammer.

It will have to do.

Steeling myself, I make my way to the door that leads to the crew bunk.

CHAPTER 28

I STEP INTO THE NARROW CABINET CONTAINING THE LADDER that leads up to the crew bunks. Behind me, the rest of the senior class is watching. I can feel the weight of their stares on my back. The old lady is with them, clearly enjoying the moment.

"The clock's running down to zero. Less than an hour now," she croaks. "You don't have much time, young Devon. Someone has to be sacrificed."

"He's the one," Spencer says softly so his voice doesn't carry up to the crew bunk. "Get him down here and he'll be our sacrifice."

Wes's face goes slack with relief. The others make noises of agreement.

But how am I supposed to do that? I have an ice hammer. Andrew and Kiara have a gun. And my mom's up there. Somehow I have to get to her and keep her safe. I need a plan, but there's no time.

I grab hold of the ladder, and my foot clangs against the bottom rung.

"Don't come up here, Devon," Kiara warns loudly, her voice tinged with hysteria. "Don't make me hurt your mother."

"Maybe I should go," Jack offers.

"No. It's my mom she's holding hostage," I say, my throat constricting.

"Stay down there. Please." It's Andrew talking this time, his voice ragged with emotion. "No one else needs to get hurt."

"You killed my sister!" I yell, my temper getting the better of me before I can stop myself.

I take a deep breath and try to recenter myself, then grab the ladder rungs again, as quietly as I can. Very, very carefully, I start climbing. It's almost impossible to be stealthy. I'm like a raging bull. All I want is to charge up there and attack. But that won't help keep my mom safe. I have to lead with my head, the way Emily would. Not with my gut.

Something rockets past, narrowly missing me before it ricochets off the cabinet wall and into the front galley. The fire extinguisher. Now I'm regretting not taking it down into the cabin earlier. What else is up there for Kiara to hurl at me? I try to remember. Pillows, blankets. Nothing lethal.

Except . . .

I'm forgetting one thing.

The flashlight.

It's at the top of the stairs.

I climb a little faster as an idea starts taking shape inside my head. I tuck the ice hammer into the waistband of my pants.

"I just want to talk," I say, working to keep my voice calm. My heart is beating so hard it feels like it might explode. "I mean, I can't hurt you, right? Because you have the gun. You have all the power. Just let me make sure my mom's okay."

There is no response. I take this as a good sign and climb the rest of the way in a hurry.

"I'm coming in," I say. "I'm going to keep my hands up so you can see them the whole time."

Very, very slowly, I ease my head through the hole in the floor and then my shoulders, then the rest of me. I keep my body turned at just the right angle so the ice hammer stays out of view. Out of the corner of my eye, I spot the flashlight, still in its charging cradle on the wall. I avoid looking at it directly, though. I don't want Andrew and Kiara to notice it's there.

They're seated on the floor beside my mom's bunk. Kiara has the gun. The muzzle is pressed against my mom's temple. Andrew is curled into himself, rocking back and forth. He doesn't look at me.

Coward.

Seeing him makes the rage inside me volcanic. It's all I can do not to erupt. But I can't yet. Not until my mom's safe. She's still unconscious, totally unaware of the danger she's in. One pull of the trigger and Kiara can end her just like that. I feel the blood drain from my head, and for a moment I feel faint.

"I don't want to hurt her," Kiara says. Her face is shiny with tears, snot running from her nose. Andrew is weeping like a little boy.

He's been hiding in plain sight all this time. Watching me and my family. Witnessing our grief. And. He. Said. *Nothing*. He hit my sister with his car and left her to die and then chose to keep it a secret to save his own skin. He is a snake. A worm. And if I can manage to pull this off, I won't feel sorry for him when the old lady possesses his body. Not one little bit.

"Why are you protecting him?" I ask Kiara. "My sister was your best friend."

Kiara's gun-holding hand starts to tremble.

"I wanted to expose him earlier, when I saw the journal in the car and realized it was his. But when I tried . . . I just couldn't. Thinking about that old lady possessing his body and him being trapped with her for eternity. That's worse than prison. That's hell, and I can't help it, I still love him," she cries, her voice tortured and miserable. "He's my person. He always has been. I couldn't sentence him to that fate. Even if he deserves it." She's crying so hard that her chest convulses. She's close to hyperventilating. The gun shifts as she struggles to regain control of herself. It's not against my mom's head but resting on the pillow beside her. Still much too close, but better.

This is my chance.

But I'm scared.

What if it doesn't work?

What if I fail?

DO IT!

Emily's voice crashes through my head, startling me into motion.

I lift the flashlight from its cradle with one hand, aim it at

Kiara's face and click it on. The bunk room is flooded with high-intensity light, bright enough to blind.

Kiara screams, stunned.

Heart racing, I reach for the ice hammer and throw it at her head. I feel Emily with me, helping to guide my hand.

My aim is off, but I still hit her—a glancing blow to her left temple hard enough to send her toppling backward. She lets go of the gun. It slides off the edge of the pillow and drops to the floor.

Covering the distance between us takes seconds, but it feels like an eternity. I can't get to that gun fast enough. Andrew is right beside Kiara. All he has to do is reach over her and grab it. He'll get there first. But he stays curled into a ball, his head tucked into the space between his knees and his chest. I drop down beside Mom and grab the gun. I aim it at Kiara.

"Don't move!" I shout.

She covers her face with her hands and starts to cry all over again. "I want to go h-h-home," she gasps. She scrambles toward the back of the bunk room and wedges herself into the corner.

I put my free hand on my mother's chest. Her heart beats steadily beneath my fingers. *She's okay. She's okay.* I repeat these words over and over to myself. I didn't realize until just now how little faith I had that my plan would work. I am weak with relief.

Andrew can't look straight at me, though. Instead, he gives me fleeting, guilty glances.

"You killed my sister." I spit the words at him.

"Yes." He nods miserably. "I know it doesn't matter, but it was an accident. I didn't see her until it was too late." He lets out a hiccupping sob. "It all happened so fast. At first I didn't even know I'd hit a person."

"Liar!" I shout. "We all saw the footage. Emily looked straight into the car."

His shoulders lift in a miserable little shrug. "It was different that night. Experiencing it in person. It was darker. Faster. Everything blurred." He shakes his head. "I thought it was a deer—or I told myself that it was. I didn't want it to be anything else, so I let myself believe it. Whenever I think about that night, I don't see Emily. I never see Emily. I see a deer. At least I did until the old lady showed that video. Now Emily's all I see."

He is trembling violently.

I shake my head. "Shut up. SHUT UP!" I don't want to hear anymore. Clouds of white mist puff out of my mouth as I talk. The bunk room is cold. Freezing.

Emily.

Her presence is everywhere. And then, impossibly, she flickers into existence beside me, transparent and ghostly, but here. Undeniably here.

I look into her face, expecting to see encouragement there, but instead there's only sadness.

Don't, she whispers inside my head.

I frown at her. Why is she saying this?

Across from me, Andrew gasps. "It's so cold." Frantically, his eyes scan the room. "Do you feel that?"

I ignore his question, and I ignore my sister, too. I need answers. And Andrew is going to give them to me. Then I'm going to take him back to the cabin to be sacrificed.

"How did you get away with it? Your windshield was shattered. There had to be dents on the hood. And all that blood. How did no one know?"

He swallows hard.

"I stopped at a car wash and sprayed off the car. It was late, so no one was there. Then I just h-h-hammered out the windshield g-g-glass. Swept it into a trash bag and put it into a d-d-dumpster." He exhales slowly and tries to calm down. "There was a dent in my hood, and one on the front bumper, but they weren't all that big. I just kept telling myself over and over and over that it was a deer. That's what I told the mechanic who fixed my car the next day too. I took it to a guy who used to come into my charity restaurant. He got hired by the garage's owner at one of our lunches, so he owed me," Andrew says. "And I don't have a reputation for being shady, so he had no reason to believe I was lying."

Kiara is crying loudly behind me. It's grating on my nerves.

My sister is hovering nearby. Flickering in and out of existence. Listening.

"You never came forward. All those months we hung out together. You saw how messed up I was. I told you and Kiara how broken my family was." I'm shaking too, but with rage, not fear. "You had a million opportunities to confess. But you never did."

Andrew curls into himself again. "I drove to the police station a dozen times," he wails. "But every time I tried to get out of my car and go in, I just froze. I couldn't get myself to do it. And I couldn't tell my parents. It would destroy them."

"Like it's destroyed my family? Whose fault is that?" I shoot back.

He whimpers. "The longer I waited to come forward, the easier and easier it got to tell myself that maybe I didn't need to. My charity was gaining traction. All those people depend on me. I convinced myself that the best way to make amends for hitting Emily was to devote myself to my work. I couldn't bring her back or change what I did. And going to jail felt like . . . I'd just be hurting more people. I figured I'd sentence myself. Keep helping others as long as I live. It's stupid and cowardly. I wanted to believe my own lies so badly." He closes his eyes and takes a shuddery breath. "But the guilt . . . it's eaten at me. I don't sleep. My grades have tanked. I've been hanging on by a thread."

"You're a miserable, selfish, worthless human being," I say.

"I know." Andrew swallows hard.

Emily watches me silently. I guess she can't manifest physically and speak to me at the same time. But her face is full of sadness, so much that I can barely stand to look at her without crying. Some of that sadness is my fault, not his. But I can make up for it. Sacrificing him won't bring her back, but it's a form of justice.

He drops to his knees. "Please, please, Devon. Don't let her possess me. I'll confess to the police. I'll go to jail. Just not that. Anything but that." He presses his hands together like he's about to pray and locks eyes with me. His are watery and red. I can smell his sweat. It makes me want to gag.

"It's too late." I grab his arm and haul him to his feet.

Emily shakes her head at me before she fades, disappears.

I aim the gun at Andrew's head. "Get up, Kiara."

She is finally quiet. Rising slowly, she walks to the ladder.

"Please," Andrew argues feebly. He is pathetic. I hate him. I hate him so much.

Stop.

Emily reappears and looks pointedly at the gun. Her hand is on mine, but I can't feel it. There is only the cold. Then she's fading again. Flickering in and out of existence faster and faster. It's like she can't maintain a semisolid form for much longer.

"I can't," I tell her. "He deserves this for what he did to you."

"Wh-who are you talking to?" Andrew asks.

I aim the gun at him.

"Just go ahead and kill me," Andrew begs. "I'd rather die here than have that thing take over my body."

"Of course you would. Because you're a coward and you're selfish. Now GET UP!" I yell the last bit so loud that he winces. I grab his arm and drag him toward the hatch in the floor.

"Do you need help?" Jack asks from the bottom of the ladder, where he's been waiting. "'Cause Carter and I will help."

Devon, no, Emily says one last time, but her voice is faint and far away and the cabin's warming up.

"I know what I'm doing," I tell her.

"Who are you talking to?" Andrew asks again, his voice going shrill.

I push Andrew toward the ladder. He holds out his hand to Kiara. She turns away.

Andrew's head droops and any fight left in him disappears. He lowers himself onto the ladder. I wait next to the hatch, aiming the gun at his head until he's all the way down, my heart beating so hard it hurts. When he reaches the bottom of the ladder, Jack seizes his arms and yanks him into the galley.

Before I leave the crew bunk, I look over at my unconscious mother. Emily is with her. Barely visible, sitting on the edge of Mom's bunk, stroking her cheek with a ghostly hand. I feel a pang of grief grip my chest. I wish Mom would wake up so she could see Emily there. But she can't. She won't until the old lady gets what she wants.

So I climb down fast, determined to make sure that she does.

CHAPTER 29

IN THE CABIN, THE REST OF THE KIDS ARE LINED UP, FACING THE aisle like a battalion of grim-faced soldiers. The old woman is at the end of the line, at the rear of the plane, standing in the center of the galley. She is so pale she glows. Her eyes shine like an animal's in the dimly lit space, and she leers at everyone—especially me—triumphantly. Seeing her glee does strange things to my stomach. I feel sick.

"Go on, go to her." I push Andrew forward. Behind me, Jack and Carter close ranks. There's no way he can turn tail and run.

The other kids scream insults.

"Murderer!"

"Liar!"

Suddenly, Spencer moves forward. He's standing taller than before, with his shoulders back. Now that we're close to finishing this, he's more like his old confident self. He spits in Andrew's face, then looks at me as if for approval. It makes me uncomfortable. I don't know how to react, so I push Andrew again, anxious to get down the aisle and get this over with.

Andrew lowers his head without even bothering to wipe the spit away. Tears pour from his eyes and splash onto the floor.

A moment later, someone throws a full soda can at Andrew. It hits him on the forehead, cutting the skin just above his left eye. Blood pours freely down his face, mixing with his tears.

Cheers erupt from the crowd.

I hear Emily's voice in my head again.

Devon. Stop.

I grip Andrew's arm a little tighter and try to steady myself.

This will all be over soon. I just need to get through the next few minutes.

Emily appears in the middle of the aisle in front of me. *Don't do this,* she says again, and this time she doesn't flicker out of existence. She's more solid than before. Her voice is so strong inside my head that every hair on my body stands up.

Don't. Do. This.

"I have to," I say.

Andrew glances back at me with bloodshot eyes.

"You see your sister, don't you? Her ghost?" He scans the cabin frantically. "I'm sorry," he whispers into the air. "I'm so, so sorry."

"Be quiet," I hiss at him. I don't understand why Emily's trying to get me to spare Andrew. It doesn't make any sense. He deserves what's about to happen. She of all people should agree with me on this.

"I don't want the old lady to possess me. I don't want to be stuck inside her forever. I know I deserve to, but I'm scared,

Devon. Please." Andrew is babbling now, stumbling down the aisle. His eyes are glued to the old woman.

Emily hovers in front of us a moment longer, her eyes wide and pleading, but her body's already slowly fading again.

When I pass Yara, she reaches out and grabs my arm. She turns her phone so I can see the screen. There's a photo of the old lady on it, taken a few minutes ago. Her energy is almost entirely yellow now, putrid and rotten, riddled with those spots. Yara raises an eyebrow. I get what she's trying to say. The old lady's body is at its weakest. There might be a way to kill her. But it doesn't matter. Andrew is getting sacrificed.

"No," I tell her softly.

Andrew kept his secret till the final hour, until his sin was revealed and he was forced to confess. If he were truly repentant, he would've come clean the second the old lady started showing everyone else's secrets. But he didn't. Because somehow, he still thought he could hide the truth and survive. He was ready to let one of us be sacrificed to save himself. Carter. Me. Spencer. Rebecca. Mai. Billy. He deserves this.

"Go on, move!" I yell so loudly that Andrew shudders.

Someone's foot juts into the aisle a moment later, and Andrew trips and falls facedown so hard I hear his teeth clack together. His phone flies out of his pants pocket and lands a few feet ahead of him. Someone stomps on it, cracking the screen.

The other kids cheer again.

I look up to see Rebecca grinning at me, her gaze conspiratorial. I yank Andrew to his feet, rage and adrenaline making me strong.

Behind me, Jack, Yara, and Carter are uncharacteristically quiet. It's obvious they're uncomfortable with what's happening, but they don't try to stop it. Kiara stumbles blindly down the aisle behind them, her face ashen. She's chewed her bottom lip to shreds. I've never seen her look so unglued, her whole body trembling. It's all she can do to keep upright. I turn back around fast. Looking at her isn't helping.

When we get to Andrew's phone, I stoop to pick it up.

His home screen has a photo on it.

It's an old picture of him with his family. His parents have him sandwiched between them and he's holding on to his younger brother. Andrew is at least ten years older than him, but the resemblance between them is remarkable. He's Andrew's mini-me. The two boys are laughing about something. The way the little guy is staring at his older brother . . . it's obvious that Andrew is his entire world.

The way Emily was mine once upon a time—that Christmas in our tree house.

The thought makes me ache inside.

Will he ever figure out that the Andrew who comes home from this trip won't be Andrew at all?

I can't help imagining this little boy living day after day with that creature squatting inside his older brother like a toad—a creature who feeds on the torment of others. What will it do to him? I'm positive he'll know Andrew isn't Andrew anymore. I'd know if it was Emily who ended up possessed. He will lose his brother even though his brother's body will be right in front of him, alive, seemingly normal. And he will never know what happened. Or why. Or how it's even possible. Andrew's brother will be just like me when I lost Emily—grief-stricken and searching for answers all alone.

Devon, don't, I tell myself. Because thinking about this messes with my anger, and I need it if I'm going to go through with this. I try to refocus, to concentrate on what Andrew's done, but the little boy's smiling face looms inside my head. It's all I can see.

Emily flickers into existence again. She looks at the screen, back at me, and shakes her head.

Stop this.

"What is it?" Jack asks.

How do I even begin to explain?

I press a hand to my chest. If I do this, won't I be like Andrew? Won't all of us? My muscles go weak. I have to fight to keep from collapsing the way Andrew did in the bunk room.

"Devon?" Jack grabs my arm to steady me.

I swallow hard and glance down the aisle to the creature. Its current body has deteriorated to nearly nothing, yet it's so powerfully alive, recharged by all the hate and violence. Recharged by *my* hate.

Emily's hand touches mine.

You can't do this, she whispers.

I stop walking and let Andrew's arm go.

CHAPTER 30

THE OTHER KIDS ARE SCREAMING AND YELLING, THEIR FERVOR reaching a fever pitch. But I can barely hear them. I can't stop staring at my sister's hand on mine.

How do I stop this? I look at Emily.

She flickers out again.

Great.

Just when I need her most.

Andrew is trembling so hard his teeth are chattering. I've never seen him so defeated. I don't want to feel sorry for him—I *don't*—but I understand now. He's not a monster so much as he's human. Awful, and a coward, but human. I want to make him out to be as bad as the creature in the old lady's body, but I can't, because I'm a coward too.

Fear is what made me run the night Emily died. Fear I wouldn't see my music dreams come true, fear that every worry my family ever had about me being a screwup is justified. And after Emily died, did I come clean to my parents? Tell them about our fight? No. I ran, and then I lied. Fear twisted Andrew, but it also twisted me. And all the rest of the kids on the plane, like Rebecca and Wes and Spencer and Billy and Mai and Carter. Fear is what drove all of us to keep our secrets. How can any of us live with what's about to happen to Andrew? Knowing what it'll do to his family?

But how can I possibly stop this thing that I've already put into motion?

That's when I remember something.

I have the gun.

I glance past Andrew at the old lady, who has been uncharacteristically quiet, so stuffed on the feast she's had of our fear and hate that she's almost dazed.

I can end this now.

I push past Andrew and run at the old woman as fast as I can. The second I'm close enough, I raise the gun and aim it at her chest.

The old lady's eyes snap back into focus. Her gaze bores into me. This time, when her mental claws scratch my brain, they manage to breach the barrier I've constructed immediately. Suddenly I feel her in me, seizing control of my hands, my legs, my brain.

Turn the gun.

Aim at yourself.

Pull the trigger.

I try to fight her off, but she's so much stronger than before. My body reacts without my consent. I feel my arm twist as if it's got a mind of its own. The hand bends inward until the gun points away from the old woman and straight at me.

"No!" Carter lunges from behind me and snatches the gun. He aims it at the old woman.

Bang!

The sound is so loud that my ears ring.

The force of the bullet hitting the old woman at such close range slams her against the rear galley wall. Blood, black and thick as tar, explodes out of her back. Actual chunks of flesh and bone land on the floor. There is a hole in the old woman's chest, directly over her heart. But instead of dying, the old bat laughs.

"I didn't think you had it in you, boy," she rasps. She glances down at her midsection. "Impressive aim."

Carter shoots again. This time he hits her in the arm. She flinches, then tilts her head from shoulder to shoulder like she's warming up for a workout.

"Well done," she says as blood oozes from the wound in her bicep. Her grin is bloody now too. I watch as a yellowed tooth falls out of her mouth. "But you'll have to do better than that if you want to get rid of me."

Carter fires again.

Click.

He stares at the gun in horror and tries again.

Click.

The gun is empty.

"Foolish boy. You were safe. All you had to do was vote for Andrew and you would've left this plane alive."

"I couldn't let you make Devon kill herself!" Carter shouts.

I stare at my best friend, tears filling my eyes. Carter is more than I deserve. He's forever trying to protect me. And I've never told him how much I love him for it. When this is over, I will.

The old woman leaps to her feet and grabs Carter so fast, it's like it happens in the blink of an eye. She turns him so he's facing all of us, his back to her. She places her bony hands on either side of his head.

"Devon?" Carter's eyes are wide and full of terror.

There is a blur of movement and then an audible snap. Carter's head twists too far to the side. His body goes boneless.

"No!" I shout.

But it's too late.

The old lady lets go of my best friend. He falls in a heap at her feet.

I can't move.

I can't scream.

Carter is dead.

CHAPTER 31

JACK WRAPS HIS ARMS AROUND ME.

I am stone beneath his touch.

"No more. I can't take all this death," I moan.

Jack holds me tighter and gently rests his head on top of my head. I feel nothing. It's like I'm not even in my body anymore. I'm floating somewhere above myself. My best friend is lying there, broken. Gone. Yara crouches beside him, weeping.

Very gently, Billy pulls her away. Spencer lifts Carter's body and settles it into an empty row of seats.

Everyone else is still lined up along the aisle, too scared to move. They're all crying. I should be crying too, but my eyes are dry. Some things are so painful you can't cry, no matter how much you want to.

"He was an idiot," Rebecca says to the old woman in a soothing voice, even as tears stream down her face. "No one wanted him to do that. Or for Devon to try to shoot you, either." She glares at me. "She's as bad as Andrew. She does whatever she wants. It doesn't matter to her how many of us die tonight. Carter never did anything wrong. He didn't deserve that."

My heart feels made of glass, cracked to the point of shattering.

"You're right," I say. "It should be me. I choose myself. I should be the one sacrificed."

The old lady's eyes light up. This is what she's wanted all along.

There's no point in fighting her anymore. My best friend died because of me. It's easier to give in now. Let the old lady take me. Save everyone else.

I start walking toward the old woman.

"Wait!" Jack cries. "We're supposed to vote. I say we vote. You said that's how it works."

The old lady's gaze lingers on my face. She wants to take me. I can feel it, the longing in her.

"We're all going to vote for Devon. So what does it matter?" Rebecca asks. "She's the only one of us who willfully endangered every person on this plane."

The crowd of kids shout their agreement.

"I'll agree to sacrifice whoever gets the most votes," Jack says. "I will. But I want every one of you to say your pick. Take responsibility for what's happening here."

"Fine," the old lady says, looking more curious than upset by Jack's suggestion. "We'll have our vote. And then I will have my new body."

She goes to Rebecca first. "Choose."

Rebecca wipes at her eyes and points at me. "Her. I choose Devon."

"Hold out your hand." The old lady pulls her knitting needles out of her pants pocket.

Rebecca obeys. The old woman drags the knitting needles down the center of Rebecca's palm. Twin trails of red well up in their wake. Rebecca hisses in pain. The knitting needles grow brighter and absorb the blood.

It's a ritual, like the kind Emily and I did when we were little. We pricked our fingers with a sewing needle and swished our blood together, sealing our fate as friends as well as twin sisters.

"And you? Choose." The old lady goes to Jeanne next. Jeanne looks at me and then Andrew before her gaze slides fleetingly to Mai and Billy. "Devon," she says finally.

"No. I should be the one," Andrew protests with more strength and conviction in his voice than I've heard in a long time. "Not Devon. Me. She was trying to do the right thing. I didn't, no matter how many opportunities I had."

The old lady draws blood from Jeanne's palm.

Two votes for me.

The old lady goes down the aisle from person to person. Kid after kid votes. My name. Andrew's. I keep the tally in my head. The vote is close. Too close.

Yara votes for Andrew.

Spencer, too.

Then Billy and Mai.

"No, it should be me," I argue, but no one seems to be listening to me or Andrew. They are focused on the old woman and her bloody knitting needles.

Kiara is next. She shakes her head, crying. "Don't make me do this," she begs the old woman. "Please, I don't want to do this."

"Choose," the old woman insists. "CHOOSE!"

Kiara lets out a yelp. "Devon."

I'm not surprised she picked me. But I *am* surprised that it hurts as much as it does. I've gotten closer to Kiara these past few months than I meant to.

The old lady goes to Jack next.

I turn to face him.

"You have to choose me," I say, the tears I've been holding back finally running freely down my face. "I can't live with Carter's death on my conscience."

Jack swallows hard. "I'm sorry, but I can't live with yours on mine." He holds his hand out to the old woman. "Andrew."

Andrew has one vote more than me. And now it's my turn.

"Choose," the old woman orders me.

I lock eyes with Andrew. Part of me wants so badly to choose him. To make him pay for Emily, even if it means hurting his family and brother. Even if it means letting myself off the hook for Carter. He nods vigorously as if he wants me to.

"Choose me. It's okay. I want you to, Devon," Andrew says with a tremulous smile.

"Me. I choose me," I say as I hold out my palm. The needles burn a path across my palm. I squeeze my hand shut. The blood pools inside my fist, then drips to the carpet.

It's Andrew's turn. I see the fear in his eyes, the lingering desire to live. The vote is tied right now. All he has to do is say my name.

"It should be me. I want it to be me," he whispers. "I vote for myself."

The choice has been made.

Majority rules.

Andrew is the sacrifice.

The old woman's eyes are feverishly bright. In her hand, the needles appear to be made of light, glowing against her skin so intensely I swear I can see every bone in her hand.

"It's settled then," she says.

"No!" I move to stand in front of Andrew, but Jack holds me back.

"It was his choice. Let him go," he says, but there are tears in his eyes. "He's trying to save your life."

Andrew nods at Jack and then closes his eyes and exhales shakily.

"Come to me, boy," the old lady says.

Weeping softly, he does.

CHAPTER 32

THE FIGHT HAS GONE OUT OF ANDREW, BUT NOT THE FEAR. THE moment he reaches the old woman, he crumples to his knees.

"Please," he says, but there's no real plea in the word. There's only surrender.

The old woman begins murmuring softly—something like words, but none I recognize. The knitting needles glow orange and yellow. The symbols appear again the way they did right before she stabbed Carlos.

She forces Andrew to look at her. Then she runs the needles over his face. They leave a bloody trail across his cheeks and forehead that moves and swirls as if the blood is a living thing. It creates a giant symbol that looks a bit like a wheel with four spokes jutting out from the center of his nose. One spoke—the shortest one—ends at his mouth, two more run the span of his cheeks to his ears, and one points directly to the top of his forehead.

"This body is mine. Its speech. Its hearing. Its thoughts. They are mine." The old woman's voice is no longer hers at all—it belongs to the one who was always just under the surface, the ancient creature living inside. The sound is like a thousand souls screaming at once. It makes my insides watery.

I watch silently from the edge of the galley. Jack is next to me in the aisle, still holding me tightly to him. Other kids have climbed into the aisle seats. Some stand on tiptoe behind us to get a better view. The only person who refuses to watch is Kiara. She's locked herself inside the bathroom in the front galley.

The old lady puts the knitting needles into her pants pocket and then shoves her fingers into Andrew's mouth. His eyes go wide as she pulls down on his bottom lip until his mouth stretches open. She uses her other hand to hold his upper jaw in place.

Andrew makes a guttural, choked sound as she forces his mouth wider still until the corners split and bleed.

Yara closes her eyes.

"I can't watch this," she says, her voice ragged, broken.

Rebecca pushes her out of the way so she can take her place and get a better view. Her eyes glint with what looks more like curiosity than horror. All her fear has melted away now that she's certain she's safe. It turns my stomach, seeing how eager she is to watch Andrew's possession.

The old lady's mouth gapes open now too. Her last remaining tooth drops to the floor and lands near my feet. The whites of her eyes have turned red with blood and her hair is literally falling out of her head, drifting to the ground like plucked goose feathers.

She makes a coughing, gagging sound. It's like she's about to be sick. Her throat bulges and stretches. Then, impossibly, something seems to climb up it.

I gasp as a black liquid the consistency of tar begins to languidly wend its way out of her, snaking through the air in a sort of looping dance. This must be the creature's real form, what it is when it's not in complete possession of a body. The old lady leans over Andrew so the black stuff slides directly into his open, waiting mouth. His arms flap uselessly at his sides as he chokes and gags. His eyes bulge and the panic there . . . it's terrifying to see.

Several kids gasp. Mai covers her face. Spencer grabs a puke bag from one of the seats and vomits into it, so hard his eyes start watering. Beside me, Jack is practically hyperventilating. And all the while, Andrew makes these awful choking noises that somehow also sound like screams.

The old lady's body starts to wither faster as the black stuff flows from her to Andrew. The skin on her fingers peels back, revealing the bone underneath. Her eyes sink into their sockets and her clothes hang on her body. The knitting needles in her pocket clink together as she diminishes more and more. She's literally wasting away before our eyes.

She's vulnerable like this.

The thought comes, loud and insistent, an alarm inside my head.

Kill her right now.

It's Emily's voice, not my own, whispering in my ear. She flickers back into existence.

Use the needles.

Except I've tried to stop her before and I've failed every time. What will make this time any different? But then I look at the needles and Emily smiles and it feels right in a way that the other times never did.

Hurry.

Again, Emily whispers inside my head. Urgent. Insistent.

I stare at the old lady and Andrew, at the black rope of the creature tethering them together, midpossession.

How do I do it? I'm only going to get this one chance.

Stab her in the throat. Pin the creature inside.

This time the words don't come from my sister, but from somewhere deep inside of me. My palm aches where the old woman cut it, where the needles made contact with my skin—as if now I'm somehow connected to them.

But what if I'm wrong?

I stare at the old woman, at her quickly dissolving body.

Then I lunge and yank the knitting needles from her pocket as I drive her backward, breaking the connection between her and Andrew. The black goo splatters all over the galley floor. I shove the old woman's head down into the mess so her neck is exposed. It's bulging and distended. The needles are hot in my hand, vibrating with power, the ancient symbols on them still glowing white. I let loose a primal scream then bring them down into the center of the old lady's neck. Her skin gives way, and the needles sink in.

The old lady lets out a strangled cry.

Her bloodied eyes stare up at me, surprised, enraged. She digs her bony, clawed hands into my back. The pain is intense and I cry out, but I don't let go of the needles. Instead, I force them deeper into her neck until I feel them hit her spine and then deeper still, until I feel them force their way between her vertebrae and out the back.

The old lady's legs kick spasmodically as her whole body shudders. She claws at me again, but this time, there is no strength left in her. Her hands flutter uselessly against my back and then her arms drop to the floor, completely depleted of strength.

I watch her breathing begin to slow.

"What did you do?" Rebecca howls. She collapses next to the old lady's body. "No, no, no. The plane's going to go down. It's going to go down and we're all going to die!" She starts pushing on the old woman's emaciated chest and then grimaces, lowers her mouth to the old woman's, and blows air into it.

"One, two, three," she murmurs to herself as she performs CPR.

Andrew is hunched over on the floor next to me, gagging and choking. He claws at his neck, his eyes wide and terrified. He can't breathe. He's suffocating. For one heart-stopping moment I worry that I was too late, that enough of the creature made its way into him. But then he retches and black gunk pours from his mouth and nose. He gasps like he's surfacing from underwater, then sags against the galley wall, spent.

I turn back to the old woman. She stares sightlessly past Rebecca, her eyes clouded over with thick cataracts. The bulge in her neck pulses rhythmically like a beating heart, and then, suddenly, it stops. The second it does, the old woman's body withers. Dries out. Turns to dust.

Disappears.

For a moment, all that remains are her clothes and the knitting needles, their glow weak and diminished. Then they disappear too.

Rebecca stares at the spot where the old woman was and screams.

There is a half-beat of utter silence before the plane free-falls.

CHAPTER 33

I FALL BACKWARD AND HIT THE SIDE OF AN AISLE SEAT SO HARD I see stars.

Everyone scrambles to grab on to something.

The creature's hold on the plane is gone. All around the cabin, the unconscious passengers begin stirring.

The plane plunges again.

The autopilot isn't working. The old lady must've disabled it. We're still in trouble.

The pilots are both dead. The only person left who can fly this plane is Mom . . . and she has no idea what she's waking up to. I have to get to her.

"Everyone, buckle up!" I yell. I pull Andrew toward our seats. He's still gasping for air, his face gray and sickly. I shove him into our row and order him to fasten his seat belt. Rebecca staggers into one of the jump seats in the galley.

"This is all your fault!" She spits the words at me as I half run, half fall down the aisle toward the front of the plane.

"What's happening? What's happening?" Mrs. Sicmaszko shrieks, fully awake now.

"Devon!" Jack calls, but there's no time to explain what I'm doing. I have to get to Mom.

Now.

Kids scramble as best they can to the closest available seat. Soda cans and alcohol bottles bounce through the cabin, pinging off the floor and seats and people as the plane falls down, down, down.

The oxygen masks drop from the ceiling.

I'm running out of time.

I reach business class as the flight attendants come to.

"Sit down!" one of them hollers at me. "Buckle up!"

I ignore her and run the last few feet to the galley, where I collide with Mom as she drops from the ladder leading to the crew bunk.

Seeing her brings tears to my eyes.

"The pilots are dead. You have to land us," I tell her.

She nods. There is confusion and panic in her eyes, but she's in control as she opens the cockpit door—even after she sees the condition of the pilots.

"We need to get him out of his seat so I can fly. Help me," she orders Shazia, who has left her seat next to Carlos to join us.

They move the first pilot to the ground and Mom climbs over him.

"What can I do?" I ask.

"Get to a seat and buckle yourself in," Mom says.

"But—"

"I need to concentrate. I can't do that if I think you're in danger. Sit down," she barks without turning around.

Shazia shuts the cockpit door, then guides me to an empty seat in business class before she grabs the mic to the PA system and buckles herself into the jump seat next to the cockpit.

Alarm bells start going off.

"Everyone, give me your attention, please. Keep your seat belts on. Bend over and put your heads down," Shazia says. "We are going to make an emergency landing."

The other adults are all awake and screaming. The two babies on board begin to howl.

"Bend over. Heads down. Stay down." The other flight attendants join Shazia and repeat these words in unison, over and in a tone so urgent it sends shivers of panic down my spine.

We are still free-falling. Is it too late? Are we still going to die?

A tremor shakes the cabin, but then, suddenly, the plane's position begins to shift. I can feel the nose struggling to pull out of the dive. Mom's doing it. She's saving us. I'm pressed down—chest to knees—scrunched too tight to breathe as the downward angle of the plane gets less and less steep.

"Come on, come on, come on," I whisper. We can't crash. Please don't let us crash. It can't end like this. I destroyed the creature. I managed to save Andrew. Carter died saving me. It can't all be for nothing. Can it? My heart contracts painfully.

A moment later, the plane levels off.

The alarm bells go silent.

Then the PA system crackles to life.

"Ladies and gentlemen, flight crew—please stay in your seats with your seat belts fastened." Mom's voice is steady, but I can still hear the thread of panic in it. She has no idea what's happened over the past four hours. I can only imagine what's going through her head.

"We are coming in for a landing," she says. "I repeat, we are coming in for a landing."

The plane starts to descend, but much more gently this time.

"Bend over. Heads down. Stay down," the flight crew chants again.

The plane banks left, then left again. Mom is heading for a safe place to land.

Most of the lights on the plane go out and we are plunged into semidarkness. I stare at the emergency exit sign, attempt to calm down, and fail. We aren't on the ground yet. Anything could still go wrong.

Outside the window, a gridwork of lights appears—a city—growing bigger every second.

Bells chime again.

"Carlos, stay with me," one of the flight crew tells the injured flight attendant. He's coughing up blood, his face a mask of panic and confusion. "We're almost on the ground."

Carlos groans in response.

The plane drops, then drops again. Outside, an airport becomes visible.

"That's not the Philly airport," Shazia mutters to the other flight attendant sitting with Carlos. "It looks like . . . Denver? We can't be here already. We just left." I see her glance down at her watch. "Wait. It's after midnight. But how?"

The lights get bigger. Buildings start coming into focus. Then a ribbon of asphalt. The tarmac. A shudder goes through the cabin as if the plane itself is breathing a sigh of relief, and then the wheels touch down with a bone-shaking jolt.

But we're okay.

We're on the ground. We're finally on the ground.

Spencer and a few other kids erupt into cheers. The adults are uncharacteristically quiet, all of them wearing matching expressions of terror and confusion. Only the babies are still howling.

The plane taxis to a stop. From somewhere outside comes the sound of sirens. Distant, but quickly growing louder.

Shazia and the other flight crew are on their feet, securing the cabin. It doesn't take them long to find Carter, obviously dead. The people around him realize he's gone at the same time the flight crew does. They start to scream as the lights come on.

I try to swallow the enormous lump in my throat.

He's really gone.

I think about his parents. What will they be told about how he died? What will the flight crew think happened to him? How can we even begin to explain?

Secret.

Emily is with me again. Inside my head.

But why? I wonder.

Secret, she whispers, more insistently this time.

After everything we've been through in the past four hours, I'm not about to argue with her. I already know that what happened on this plane for the last four hours has to stay a secret. But it feels like a betrayal. Carter was a hero in the last minutes of his life and now only us Greendale kids will ever know that.

"Ladies and gentleman, we will be evacuating the plane immediately. One row at a time. Please stay buckled in your seats until we tell you to get up," Shazia says over the PA system. She looks as shell-shocked as I feel.

She walks to my row and tries to get me to move to the exit.

"Not without my mom," I tell her.

She starts to argue and I snap.

"I'm not leaving this plane without her. Evacuate everyone else."

Something about my expression makes her leave me alone.

While I wait for Mom to emerge from the cockpit, I watch as our chaperones, along with a few other adults, are recruited to help the flight crew with evacuation. The emergency doors on the wings are opened. The inflatable slides are deployed. It's strange how tense they all are, like somehow the threat is still present when it's not. The old lady is gone, but none of the adults know that. The past four hours are a total blank space for them. Still, they manage to leave the plane in an orderly fashion, clinging tightly to one another as they wait their turn to go down the slide. If they knew what really happened, they'd be diving out of this plane.

The next few minutes are a blur of activity.

Row by row, the passengers are evacuated. It seems to happen painfully slowly. In reality, it's probably only minutes. I just want off this plane. The walls feel closer and closer all the time—

like I'm sealed inside a metal casket. But I'm not leaving without Mom. I abandoned Emily on Halloween. I won't abandon my mother.

When the plane is nearly empty, the cockpit door opens.

"Why aren't you on the tarmac with everyone else?" Mom asks.

"I wanted to go with you."

She looks at me, really looks at me, at the blood on my clothes, at the scratches the old lady left on my skin when we fought. "What happened up there?"

What is it about moms? One minute you're holding it together, the next they're asking one measly question and it's like they've pulled the rip cord on your emotions.

I burst into tears.

"Honey, are you hurt? Show me where." She places her hands on both my cheeks and searches my eyes.

I shake my head because I'm crying too hard to answer.

Mom starts to guide me toward the exit. "We need to get off the plane, and then I want you to tell me what happened, okay? Once you're safe."

My breath hitches as I try to rein in my tears.

"It's your turn. Go on," Mom urges when I'm finally standing in the doorway, the ramp billowing out beneath me. Below, nearly all the passengers are gathered by a collection of emergency vehicles. This is it. It's finally over.

But I can't make myself move.

"Sit down and push off. I'll be right behind you." Mom puts her hand on my back.

"There's something I need to tell you," I say.

"We have to get off the plane. You can tell me once you're safe," she says.

"No. Now."

Mom frowns.

"The night Emily died we had a fight. You sent her to get me and drive me home. I was mad because I thought she told you about me skipping classes, so I wouldn't give her the keys. And I told her to walk home. I said I hoped she'd freeze to death."

Mom inhales sharply, and I want to crawl under the nearest seat and die.

There is one unbearable moment of silence, and then Mom pulls me close and wraps me in her arms. We're heart to heart and cheek to cheek, and it's been so long since I've let her hold me this way. It's been forever.

"Her death was not your fault. You were angry and you said some awful things, but she knew you didn't mean them, not really." Mom's voice is strained, full of emotion. "You loved your sister and she loved you. I'm so sorry you've been holding that in all this time. Because it doesn't change how I feel about you. I love you. So, so much." She starts to cry. "And whatever happened here tonight, I'm so glad that I didn't lose you too."

"I love you," I tell her, because I never say it enough. Not to her. Not to Emily. And they both deserved to hear it more. They deserved to hear it all the time.

Mom gently disentangles herself from me and pushes me toward the bright yellow slide again. "You have to go now. Sit down and lean back."

I sit. I lean. Then I close my eyes and slide. There is a rush of frigid air against my face, and then my feet touch tarmac. I am on the ground, out of the plane. The relief is overwhelming. I smile as Mom lands beside me. It's really over. We survived. We're free.

A second later, I'm being ushered away to where the rest of my classmates are huddled, wide-eyed and silent. They stand apart from the adults, in their own section of the runway.

Yara rushes up to me.

"Look." She thrusts her phone into my hand.

The camera app is open. All her photos and videos are lined up on-screen. The last batch is from yesterday. I stare at the date listed at the top and frown.

"Why did you delete the ones from the plane?"

Yara shakes her head. "I didn't. They weren't here when I went to pull them up so I could show the police."

Secret. Emily's last word to me reverberates through my head.

Did she wipe Yara's phone? Or did the old woman somehow do it?

I listen for my sister's voice, wait for her presence to descend on me the way it has for the past four hours, but there is nothing.

"We don't know anything. We don't remember anything. No matter what," I tell the other kids when it's safe enough for us to talk without being overheard. No one can learn what really happened up there. They wouldn't believe us, not without proof. We will pretend we were unconscious too, just like the others. We will act like we don't know what happened to Carter or the old lady or the plane. It's the only way, now that Yara's photos and videos are gone.

The others nod one by one. It should make me feel better that we're united, but it doesn't. Tonight is a new secret we have to keep. And it's a heavy burden, one we have no choice but to carry.

When Jack and I finally get a minute together, he gathers me in his arms and hugs me tight. "You saved us," he whispers into my hair before he plants a soft kiss on top of my head.

"Not all of us," I whisper.

I glance back at the plane. For some reason I feel myself drawn to the back windows. Two people appear to be looking out.

I suck in a breath.

One of them is Carter.

The other is Emily.

They each press a hand to the glass and stare out at me. Somehow I know it is the last time I will see them.

This is goodbye.

There is so much to say. So many things I want them to know. But death doesn't care about the things we neglect to tell each other when we have the time.

All I can do is wave as they disappear.

THE NEXT DAY

CHAPTER 34

THE NEXT TWENTY-FOUR HOURS ARE A BLUR. THEY KEPT US AT the airport for what seemed like forever. I was questioned several times—we all were—but everyone stuck to the story we agreed on. All we remember is the old woman stabbing Carlos, and then, shortly after, the cabin filling up with gas.

But there are a lot of unanswered questions.

Too many. Especially about Carter.

I know the people investigating what happened on Flight 171 will contact me again. It's only a matter of time. But when they do, I still won't have much to say.

So far, the TSA and the FBI both seem to think it was some sort of terrorist attack. They've asked if the old woman said anything that sounded like a threat. And they're searching for her. Right now, they're probably busy going through an apartment that matches the address she used when she purchased her ticket.

Now I'm sitting by the large fireplace at our resort. It's just as perfectly cozy as it was in the brochure photo. Jack and Yara are with me. We'll only be here for a few hours—just until the bus our parents chartered arrives to take us back to Pennsylvania. The only place any of us wants to be is home. And there is no way in hell we're getting back on a plane.

Yara stares into the fire and sighs.

"I don't know how to be after this."

"Me neither," Jack says. "I keep getting flashes of all of it. Of Carter." His gaze flicks to me. "How are you doing?"

"I don't know," I admit. And it's the truth. I don't. "I can't believe he's actually gone. The more hours that go by, the more the whole flight feels like a nightmare—absurd and unreal. I keep expecting Carter to plop down next to me and do an impersonation and then make me guess which famous actor it is."

Yara leans forward and rests her elbows on her knees. She's got her phone cradled in her hands, screen side up so we can see.

"I Googled her. The old woman. Dorothy Burdon." She keeps her voice low so no one but us will hear.

"What did you find?" Jack asks.

"Nothing at first. I mean, her address and a phone number. But otherwise, she's like a complete ghost. But when I went through Google Images, I found this."

I stare at the picture on-screen. It's of a group of girls huddled in the snow, standing alongside a train. The image is black-and-white. The girls in it are all wearing old-fashioned school uniforms, and they have their hair styled in pin curls.

They're staring unsmiling at the camera—all except one very pretty girl on the right-hand side. She's standing just slightly apart from the others, leaning in toward the camera. She isn't smiling, exactly, but there is a twinkle in her eye. It feels like she's looking straight out of the picture at me. Like she's alive inside the photo somehow and knows I'm looking at her. The other girls have their shoulders angled away from this girl, as if they're trying to create a subtle barrier between themselves and her.

It's her eyes that give her away. Intense and powerful. Unforgettable.

The old woman from the plane.

Yara clicks on the link beneath the image. It brings up a newspaper article. The headline reads: "Train Crossing the Rockies Narrowly Avoids an Avalanche. Four Passengers Remain Unaccounted For."

The article goes on to describe how the avalanche happened in the middle of the night, blocking the train's path. It was bound for the West Coast. The passengers were sleeping. Most of them never even woke when the train was forced to stop. There was a group of girls from a private college traveling home for the holidays on the train. By morning, three of them were missing. Since the avalanche managed to avoid the train entirely, it was the theory of the conductor, as well as the other schoolgirls, that the missing young women and an elderly man, one Albert Marshall, must have wandered outside the train after it stopped and gotten lost. Search parties were organized, but after several days they were called off and those missing were presumed dead. Conditions were much too harsh for any of them to have survived longer than that.

When asked why she thought her friends would wander out in the snow in the dark, eighteen-year-old Dorothy Burdon had this to say: "I believe they did it on a dare," she said. "They were like that, those girls, always taking risks. Doing bad things."

"Oh my God," I breathe. I go back to the photo and zoom in. There is no mistaking it this close. It really is Dorothy. Her name is at the bottom of the image along with the other girls'. There are twelve of them total. I read each of the other girls' names out loud.

"I wonder what their secret sins were," I murmur. I trace a finger over Dorothy's face. When the picture was taken, was the real Dorothy still there somehow? Aware, but trapped somewhere inside her head? Looking out her own eyes like the windows of a prison, forced to observe, but never able to speak or be heard ever again? I glance down at the hands of the girls in the photo. Every single girl has hers balled into fists, so I can't see the cuts across their palms; still, I know they are there. I open my own hand and stare at the gash. It's sealed up, more pink than red and healing more rapidly than it should. Still, I can feel it, like a burn—or a brand.

Where are these girls today? They'd all be old ladies in their nineties. I wonder how their lives have been in all the years between then and now. How have they managed to live with themselves all this time with Dorothy out there somewhere, possessed? I take out my own phone and Google the name of the first girl listed. Imogen Churchill. The only thing that pops up is an obituary. Imogen Churchill: Born July 10, 1930. Died March 2, 1948. Only a year after the train incident. I stare at the Imogen on Yara's phone. Then I Google the next girl listed: Hazel Pierce. A newspaper article for a place called Wilke's Corners comes up. Headline: "Local Swimming Star Drowns." Dated August 25, 1948. Six months after the first girl died.

"What?" Jack asks, moving so he's beside me and can look over my shoulder at my phone.

"The girls on the train with Dorothy. The first two I looked up died about a year after. Within six months of each other." I Google the next name: Ruth Williams. This one gets a few more hits, but only because Ruth won a national essay contest sponsored by the White House the year before the train incident. There are several articles written about it as well as a few photos of her shaking hands with President Truman. Her obituary is the third link listed. She died December 13, 1948.

A cold chill runs down my spine.

"It could be a coincidence," Jack says, but there's no conviction in his words. He doesn't believe it any more than I do.

"She was going to kill us no matter what," Yara whispers. "The second she chose us, we were all going to die. Sacrificing someone wouldn't have saved any of us, not really. It would've damned us— if she'd lived."

"But she didn't. Devon destroyed her—it, whatever it was." Jack grabs my hand and squeezes. "We're safe."

He's right. It makes sense that he's right. How can the creature come for us if it's gone? But still, my body breaks out into goose bumps. I open my palm and stare down at the angry red line at the center again. We sealed our fate when we made our choice and she cut us. If I hadn't killed her, we would only have a few more months to live.

"But why go after the others?" Yara asks. "After it possessed Dorothy. It doesn't make sense."

"It's how she stayed fed." I don't know why I say it. It just sort of pops into my head, almost like it's not my thought at all. "It's like spiders. How they bite some of their prey just to paralyze them, then save them for later when they get hungry."

I shiver. It's a horrific thought, so to distract myself I look out the large floor-to-ceiling window facing the ski slopes and watch the skiers weave their way down. The world outside is so bright I need to squint to see it. For the first time since Halloween, I feel like maybe everything is going to be okay. The creature's dead, and even though Emily isn't with me, I know she isn't gone, either. There is more after this life. Knowing that makes it easier to let her go. To leave this place, this moment, and never look back.

CHAPTER 35

IT'S JUST AFTER SUNSET WHEN WE FINALLY BOARD THE BUS FOR home.

I stare out at the gray evening sky, rife with snow clouds, and exhale heavily enough to fog up the window beside me, so I can draw with my finger in the steam. A circle with four spokes. I stare at it for a long moment, then wipe it away before anyone can see.

Yara's got the seat beside me, and Jack is behind us. He's already asleep, his head resting on the backpack he's wedged next to the window to create a makeshift pillow.

The heater is on, and the air is cozy and warm. It makes me feel drowsy too.

Mom sends me a quick text to check in. She's still helping Sky Royal figure out what happened on Flight 171 and won't be home for another day or two. I miss her already, but maybe it's better to have a little time to process everything on my own. I text her back and tell her I love her for the tenth time today.

Yara flips through a book she bought in the hotel store. It's a rom-com with a cotton-candy-pink cover.

"Since when are you into romance?" I shake my head and laugh at the sappy couple on the front of the book staring dreamily at each other.

"Yeah, I might be done with horror—like, for the rest of my life," she says, shivering. It surprises a laugh out of me. Yara smiles, then starts giggling too.

Things aren't exactly normal yet, but I can feel them moving in that direction.

I watch Spencer board the bus with Billy. They are uncharacteristically quiet. Spencer glances back at me as he slides into his seat. He looks ragged, hollowed out, but still, he manages to smile at me. I smile back.

Jeanne boards next and slips into the seat behind the driver, jamming her AirPods into her ears and staring intently out the window. She's been avoiding all of us since we left the airport.

Mai slips in with Kiara next. They stay up front too, close to Mrs. Sicmaszko. Kiara barely seems to notice where she is. She hasn't said a word since last night. It's like she's catatonic. Mai smooths Kiara's hair away from her face and talks to her, words I'm too far away to hear. She's traded taking care of Jeanne for taking care of Kiara, it seems. Maybe that's for the best. I don't think Kiara and I will still be friends after this.

The bus is big enough to hold more than fifty people, so there is plenty of room to spread out. Even so, I have to keep looking out the windows because the bus interior is too much like the plane's—all aisle and seats. I keep getting flashes of the old woman scrambling across the ceiling, her eyes glowing, and that grin, that awful grin.

We're safe, I remind myself over and over.

Wes and Mr. Lewton board next and make their way to the back of the bus, as far from Spencer as possible. Wes confessed what he did, right after he got off the plane. And when he gets back, he's going to turn himself in to the police.

I press my face to the glass. Andrew hasn't boarded yet. I haven't seen him since the plane.

"His parents flew in earlier," Yara whispers. "I saw them arrive. I think he's already told them what he did."

Something inside me that's been clenched like a fist since the night my sister died releases, but it's weird. I don't feel vindicated like I thought I would. So many lives were devastated that night. It's the kind of damage that leaves a permanent wound, even if justice is served.

The bus driver honks the horn as a last call for any stragglers.

Rebecca climbs on board, her cheeks red with cold. Once she's in, the bus doors swing shut. Everyone who's supposed to be on the bus is here. Time to go.

I hug my jacket to my chest and rest my head against the seat.

Outside, snow starts to fall—big fluffy flakes that collect at the corners of my window.

Rebecca makes her way down the aisle to an open spot a few rows up. She tosses her backpack onto the seat. Of all of us, she seems to have rallied the fastest. Ever since we landed, she's been back to her old self, bubbly and talkative. In the hotel lobby earlier, she was even flirting with one of the ski instructors. It's like she's blocked out everything that happened last night, even if her palm—and her mouth—still bears the injuries from it.

I watch her take off her coat and fold it neatly. She's humming softly to herself, too low for me to make out the tune. Something about it sends a chill through me. I have a sudden, overwhelming sense of déjà vu. I lean forward as Rebecca bends down to retie the laces on her snow boots. There's something sticking out of one of them. A pair of sticks.

My breath catches.

Not sticks.

Needles.

Knitting needles.

I stand up in my seat.

It can't be. I'm seeing things. It's impossible. The creature poured itself into Andrew, not Rebecca. But then I have a flash of memory, a fleeting image of her leaning over the old woman's body to give her CPR. She put her mouth on the old woman's. The plane was falling. Is it possible in that moment Rebecca was so afraid she offered herself up to the old woman to keep her from crashing the plane?

As if sensing my stare, Rebecca turns her head slightly. I watch as the corners of her mouth turn up in a smile. For one brief second, her eyes seem to catch the light from outside and glow.

No, no, no.

I shut my eyes tight. Please, please don't be real.

Don't be real.

When I open my eyes, the needles are gone. I remember how to breathe again.

They weren't there at all, I tell myself. *You're having some kind of post-traumatic episode. That's it. It has to be.*

"What is it?" Yara tugs gently on my sleeve.

"Nothing." I shake my head to try to clear it. The creature is dead. I killed it. And the needles disappeared when it did. It's impossible for Rebecca to have them, right?

Right?

The bus rumbles to life. I'm knocked back into my seat as it lurches forward and trundles down the winding road that leads away from the lodge, into the night.

ACKNOWLEDGMENTS

A successful flight (or book) is dependent on its crew. I am so grateful for the talented group of people who worked on this one.

First, thank you to my husband and daughters, who have supported me and patiently put up with my erratic work hours and endless daydreaming. I wouldn't have the courage to tell my stories if you didn't believe in my ability to do it. I love you guys.

Christina Farley, this book wouldn't exist without you. Thank you for thinking of me when you saw Wendy's tweet requesting horror pitches for Underlined. I am truly in your debt. And an extra big hug to you and Vivi Barnes for gamely reading from rough pitch to final draft. You both gave so many critical insights to make it better, even though neither of you are horror fans and you lost sleep in the process!

Much love and appreciation to my agent, Lucienne Diver. It's been six years since my last published novel. You never wavered in your support of me. I can't find words for how much this means to me. I'm so lucky to work with you.

Wendy Loggia, you are my fairy godmother. Thank you for choosing *Flight 171* for your list. You breathed new life into my career. I will always be grateful to you for helping me make my dreams come true.

Hannah Hill, thank you for loving this book and putting so much passion into it. You have made it infinitely better. I pinch myself all the time that I get to work with such an amazing editor who seems to know the inner workings of this story (and my brain) even better than I do.

A round of applause as well to designers Casey Moses, Sophia Chunn, and Cathy Bobak. This story is "dressed" for success because of you.

Lastly, thank you to all the readers out there who give this book and me a chance. I hope you enjoy it.

ABOUT THE AUTHOR

AMY CHRISTINE PARKER is the author of *Gated, Astray,* and *Smash & Grab.* She writes full-time from her home near Tampa, where she lives with her husband and their two daughters.

amychristineparker.com